Sink on Impact

NICK WESTFALL

Strategic Book Group

Copyright © 2011

All rights reserved—Nick Westfall

No part of this book may be reproduced or transmitted in any form or by any means, graphic, electronic, or mechanical, including photocopying, recording, taping, or by any information storage retrieval system, without the permission, in writing, from the publisher.

Strategic Book Group
P.O. Box 333
Durham, CT 06422

www.StrategicBookClub.com

ISBN: 978-1-61204-436-1

Dedicated to Jacob Babb

In loving memory of Adam Gerken

Epilogue

A MEMORY, A FACE, AN IMAGE

I WATCHED MYSELF fade away from hands that continued to remain distant. I was drifting into an unwarranted abyss. When I faced my fate, I slowly fell to the bottom. They put the cement that lay dehydrated around my feet. What they didn't know was that I knew a way out. I could have escaped this death. Instead, I sunk at the will of my own. With a released jaw and nothing to repent, I opened my lungs to the truth that swallowed me. Gradually, I felt my senses fail simultaneously.

There was always a moment that you never wanted to end. Instead of cherishing that moment, I thought about all of the ways I could have prevented it from stopping. I needed to release this tension. Jesse would have let go. He would allow that one moment to reach its full potential and wouldn't fight them barging in to take him. They gave me time. They could have just come in and ripped me apart.

It was the same conglomerate who killed Jesse. All of them played a part in it. Even the one who took him out of the car that final night Jesse was alive. They were a gang of killers. Each person had their own agenda with Jesse. I wanted to make sure that they knew what they had done. I was going to get to them, before they got to anyone else. Pain like this heals but never goes away. I still see his face. It follows me everywhere I look and in everyone I see.

Jesse was in all of these people. As a role model, he inspired others, creating a population based on morals and honesty. Truth was something that we all had forgotten. If it wasn't for Jesse, we could have never aimed to regain that purity.

The majority of people lose their honesty when they are young. Jesse was one of those rare beings who skipped the part where he was supposed to lose his innocence. He was a walking paradigm of what we all wanted to be, and by touching his life, we became better people. Without a pillar like Jesse, many people never recapture the truth and innocence of their youth.

Jesse was a true go-getter. When he did something, he did it well. He had a profound desire to become a teacher. I didn't know much about him in high school, but in college he made superior grades that left professors in shambles because he became smarter than they were.

In many ways I can only aspire to be like him. I am the eighty percent guy. I love to start extravagant ideas, and that's usually where they stay, at the start. Jesse was more than a role model for me, he was an idea. His vision would change everything wrong in the world. It would be a perfect place, a real Utopia. He was murdered at the wake of his vision.

Jesse constantly struggled to please the people he loved. *He was a blissful person, so how could it end like this?* I have to help him. I will prove all the naysayers wrong. I will make an exception to my usual eighty percent tendency and finish what he started because this is the story that he can't tell you. This is the dark side of the moon. This is the brutal path of righteousness, among a list that could have ended it before this all happened. Life took him for ransom, and all *they* wanted was someone to give *them* a reason to stop.

Chapter 1

IT WAS ALL happening too fast, and my eyes couldn't maintain the speed. I was falling asleep and sliding around in my seat. I felt sick. We were having so much fun before she ruined it. The seat felt cold and slick, and my stomach was flipping in knots. With every turn he took, I could feel my body's nausea state slowly worsening. No matter what happens, I will remember how happy I was that he decided to come with me. I wasn't going to let her rain on my parade.

Clutching a paper bag, my stomach's contraction broke as the contents of my day unfolded. All of the colors in the paper bag became a guessing game to determine which one was breakfast, lunch, or dinner. The purple must have been from the Captain Crunch Berries cereal I had this morning. The orange was the cheese puffs I had for lunch. And the overwhelming, uninviting color of brown must have been the Jaeger Bombs chased with beer. *What can you expect of a college graduate? It was a night I patiently waited to take part of.*

I didn't feel better after it happened like I normally did. I was physically drained from the extended workout my gag reflexes just accomplished. My eyes slowly closed. I hated that when I needed to stay up I had to fight sleep, but whenever I wanted to go to sleep it never happened. I needed to stay awake because it was too risky for me to lie down. We should not have been driving this late because we knew they surrounded this area at night.

I attempted to think about something else, but all I thought about was what would happen if they caught us. It would be the end of our lives. We were scared and there was no way to hide it. On our faces were masks projecting calm, cool, and collected expressions, with the truth of fear and the fear of truth oozing through the cracks around the edges. The scenery outside the window started to spin faster than my eyes could handle. Everything was a blur, and I still had more contents to add to my warm, colorful paper bag.

Minutes later, I finally began to feel like myself again. Although my buzz was gone, I tried to picture myself being a better person. I wanted to be someone like Jesse who always strived to find ways to improve the world. He had so much affection for people. He loved people he didn't even know. I wanted to be able to look at people the way he did. He honored before he judged. That has become a scarce quality in people today.

He kept on driving the car, and I continued to fill my paper bag. It started to leak and there wasn't room for more. I wanted to tell him to stop the car so I could politely vomit out of the window without getting any of it in my car.

I wouldn't know how to ask him. I didn't know Jesse that well, or maybe I didn't know Jesse the way I really wanted to know him. I had only known him for a little over a year. He was assigned to me. I wanted to show him all of the things he was missing by staying inside and doing nothing at night. He needed to be out more. *I knew this was good for him.* No one has a desire to be inside an apartment *forever*.

He was great at putting on a façade. Only his friends knew when he wasn't himself. It was easy to tell once you got to know him. He only branched out and started conversations after he knew people well. He was usually a quiet person, but when something was bothering him he was as silent as the walls in the room. When you didn't hear from him, it meant there was something wrong. Tonight was me reaching out to him. *He needed this, right?*

He became mute. I had to say something to make sure he was aware of the severity of our situation.

"Jesse, come on man. Stop worrying about her, dude."

He was so pathetic sometimes. His womanly attitude was the whole reason we left. We weren't supposed to leave yet. I wanted him to meet more people.

"Just remember you're driving my car," my selfish reminder that neither of us should be driving in this part of town at this time of night.

"I know."

He was so confident when he said those words. He was good at making me feel secure with him driving my car. He constantly looked down in the beginning of our friendship and said things that seemed more like a question than a response. After all of the time we spent together, it wasn't until recently that he revealed the confidence in himself through his words. His confidence could only be seen by the ones he trusted, because he never wanted to be mistaken for someone he was not. He aimed to please even the people that he did not know. He would help people who could not help him, and that was a trait of his that I desperately wanted to gain. I have never helped anyone who had nothing to offer me.

I drove a white 2006 Lexus IS300. Jesse constantly reminded me my expenses were higher than my income. His metaphor for my income revenue was a Styrofoam cup. The sand he poured into it was my income. Normally, people had expenses represented by one hole that slowly leaked out the income pouring in.

My revenue, he said, and I quote, "You don't have a bottom to your cup. It all just comes straight down."

I responded, "Are you going to clean off the floor?"

I said that just to make us laugh. I tried to do that a lot. Even though Jesse was always happy, or at least pretending to be, I could tell he needed to laugh every once in a while.

"She's a bitch, man. There's nothing else to it. Let her go out with her tax write-off friends."

I knew that would make us both relax. It was good comic relief.

He started to grin. Seeing his smile assured me that we were going to be all right, even in this dangerous state of affairs. I tried to reach for the stereo, because he hit pause while we were talking. Then the worst thing that could ever happen, happened.

Oh my God.

We were so close to home, and we knew the death of both of us was getting ready to take place. *You've got to be kidding me! Please no. Not now. Pleeeeeeaaasssee.*

"Oh God!"

This isn't real. No, wake up! Come on, this can't be happening.

When I saw his unfamiliar emotions spill out I could tell this was real.

"No. No. No."

He repeated to himself in an echo that spoke louder than his previous words. The car stopped immediately. We both knew what was about to happen and our futures were at stake. *We had to run.* I slammed the dashboard, making two symmetrical impressions on the leather. We were so damn close to home.

Not now. *Why?*

When you play with fire you are bound to get burned. Those are the statistics.

Chapter 2

IT'S NOT ABOUT the life you lead, but whose life you helped by the end. The world through Jesse's eyes has shown me that it's more important to care for other people before myself. *Why did the people on the list leave him to die? All he needed was someone to show him they cared. He would still be here if they would have been there for him.* I know I am placing the blame on others for a situation we both could have avoided; but it was their need for him to suffer that killed him. They all had a hand around his neck in this case.

He was neither a friend nor an enemy, but merely someone who I can say I cared for and with whom I empathized. I know there are certain things that he could have done differently, but I still stand by him. I felt what he felt. I know the people on the list were given the control to stop this and they didn't. I also know that they were the ones who got us into this disaster. *Why was he alone? Why didn't anyone get the call? I had all of these questions. I had to find the right questions to lead me to the right answers.* There were things that needed to be addressed so this case could be resolved, and we could all agree on what happened on that terrible night.

In my newly created line of work, I became the victim to understand why events played out the way they did. I had to experience the crime to comprehend the possibilities of what could have happened. This job was not paid in money; instead, I was paid by the ability to solve the case with no regrets. Like anyone who starts a new career, I put all of my energy into being the best candidate I could have been for the job. It had to be done. The hardest part of the job was convincing *them* Jesse was murdered. Although it wasn't the only motive for completing this case, I found myself questioning my continuance in Jesse's murder. They all cried that it was an accident. I disagreed.

I was greatly influenced by my new job because I felt the need to see the death of a victim through the holes in their skull. Influences came from the information the suspects gave me. In order to look through the eyes of the dead, I have to see Jesse through their perception while keeping my own opinion of him at bay. It's like a mirror. I had to see what they saw. I wouldn't know who Jesse was unless I knew who he was to all of them, even the ones who killed him.

I loved this case. This one was personal and way too close to home. I had to experience the true death of a suspect, and a friend. I think that's why I loved this investigation. Pieces of me were in every one of those responsible. I died when Jesse died. My happiness flaked away when I saw his face.

Chapter 3

THERE WAS A young man driving down campus in a very clean car, sticking his head out of the window into the sobering air. He searched for ways to stop thinking about what happened that night. It was very late and he should not have been driving.

He thought to himself, "I hope he's okay. I wonder where they took him. Is this my fault?"

The young man doesn't know his roommate too well, so he was confused as to what he needed to do to correct this situation. The more he thought about ways to rectify it, the higher the guilt rose inside him.

He tried to think about graduation and how happy he was the day everything centered on him. It took him longer to finish than most students, but he did it. He even took the liberty of taking a bow on the stage after accepting his diploma; making everyone in the Greensboro Coliseum cry out in laughter. He tried very hard to make people smile by telling jokes. He wanted everyone to think he was funny.

His mom gave him the biggest hug a mom could give. She was the proudest mother in the stands. Real men shouldn't cry, he thought. But that day there was something about that hug. It wasn't like he never had a hug like that before. He had plenty of hugs from her. He thought the world of his mother. She was a very sweet woman and they had been through a lot, but the young man didn't want to think about anything negative at that particular moment. He just walked away from a negative situation, and he hoped that everything would be back to normal in the morning. In the back of his mind, he knew that everything changed. Nothing would be the way it was before.

The car began to swerve, and he knew that he should not have been driving this late. He drove up to the light and waited for it to turn to yellow, then red. The car had an automatic transmission, but the young man played with the shift knob like it was a manual. Like the shift knob, he slid side to side with his thoughts jumping from one to another and back again.

He forced himself to think of a happy time before that night as the light returned from the cycle back to green.

He's sitting in a room with his mother playing Scrabble. His mother, being forty-eight years old, has a lot more recollection and exposure to many different words. She was the Scrabble queen of their small family. His mother had a natural ability to see his future moves as she prepared her next move. She set her son up with at least two vowels in each one of her words so he could easily add to the board. She knew he would quit if he had to repeatedly skip a turn to trade in his letters for new ones from the pile. It was like she had a plan to save him from the start of the game.

In the room where they played, the temperature seemed perfect to him. It wasn't too hot or too cold. He was wearing a red thermal shirt and jeans. Wearing the same layers of clothing, she had to keep going outside of the house to get some of the sharp winter air. This happened enough for him to notice. He started to grin because he knew what was going on. Before she came back in the house, he thought of all of the ways he could use the word "hot."

When she returned and asked where he placed his word, he said,

"I've got a real scorcher here."

He held in his laughter until she showed him she understood his joke. She placed down the word "score." Almost upset that there wasn't a way to manipulate the word score, he decided to up his game.

He used his "H" and "T" and completed a wasted elementary word using her "O." She started to smile, showing him signs she understood the joke. He took off his thermal, leaving only a short-sleeve shirt.

"Is it HOT in here to you?"

They both shared a laugh and continued to play, even though the young man was not done with the joke yet. He still had more. He needed one last kicker, something that wasn't too obvious and took a little thought on her part. He got his idea and excused himself from the board. He walked to the refrigerator and took out a bag of fruit. They both loved fruit. As a child, he only ate fruit if it was cut up, and this bag had a variety of slices. He walked back in the room holding his emotions together. He knew that they both would get a kick out of this one. She was outside again getting some more of that winter air.

When she came back he was eating an orange slice and replenishing the letter pieces he just used onto his holder. She sat back down and looked down at the new word on the board and thought about a longer word that would hopefully leave her son with multiple opportunities to place more words down.

"Fruit?" he asked.

"No, I'm all right. Thank you though."

He prepared his punch line. "Are you sure? They've been in the refrigerator, and they're very cold."

Both of them slowly burst into laughter like when the stadium security guys finally give up trying to keep the celebratory fans from getting on the court.

He continued with the jokes and she didn't mind, but the hot and cold jokes were starting to get old, and she wanted to politely tell him to stop. He wanted to keep her laughing. He loved the time he could spend with her because she was all he had and they had been through a lot. After they cleaned up the Scrabble game he began to think about ways to manipulate the word "flash." He was going to say …

The young man slammed on the brakes as the stop sign slowly slid past the car, from the front windshield, to the passenger-side windows, and finally the back corner of the rear windshield. Screeching tires and sweat drops commenced before a breath of relief exhaled through his mouth. He knew that he could not think about things too deeply because he needed to pay attention to what was in front of him. Luckily, it was four in the morning and traffic was light. Only the very small group of early morning risers and policeman were out at this time.

He reminded himself why he was driving, and he served himself a plate of responsibility with a side of enragement. Vindication couldn't describe how conflicted the young man felt. He pulled over at a gas station and started to question himself again. He debated whether he should go back or not.

'I hope he's going to be all right. Please be okay, Jesse.'

Chapter 4

I MISS HIM so much. I can't feel anything but anger. When everyone points the finger, it only makes it worse. Their words get through my protective barrier. Instead of taking the easy route and feeling sorry for myself, I infuriate myself. I will destroy them all. They'll be drowning in the frozen lake screaming for help and asking for forgiveness. I watch as the undertow takes them, then I walk away because I put them there.

I took Jesse's ability to put on a mask for people. They saw a concerned college graduate searching for his friend's past. They didn't have a clue what kind of fire was burning inside of me. Not only was I going to find the murderers, I was going to slit their throats one by one. Slit their throats so deep that it pierces all of the nerves in their necks, creating a permanent smile from ear to ear. I will watch them as the blood pauses before spilling out over the lower extremities. I want to see the sensitive skin break on their necks. The investigation was fueled by my desire to see their emotions spilling out before their blood runs down, thus exposing the fierceness of my anger to them.

I wasn't trying to make them like me; instead I was trying to persuade them to let me into their thoughts. I needed to feel the inside of their confession to touch their point of view. I had to make sure it was honest. I didn't want anything except the truth. My life stopped when he was killed that night. The obscurity of his death was the only motivation that kept me alive.

The tragic image of his face brought new thoughts. I started to become intrigued by death. Seemingly, death never ends. For death is the only true forever. There is no coming back from death. There is no option of restarting and trying again. Once you're dead, you are dead forever. And forever is a question without an answer. Forever is neither measured by time but a representation of time that starts and never ends. Life is ever-changing and has multiple paths of choice. But death is an unchanged infinite. Death is a line ray.

I had a mystery to solve through an investigation that wasn't going to be enjoyable for either party. The truth is, there is no happiness in death, unless death is an end to a suffering. Jesse was not suffering. At least that was what we all thought.

I had numerous theories about who would be held responsible for his death. *Who was the one that brought him to his end?* I thought I knew that answer, but I was still looking for something else. I was looking for reasons to believe there was something I was missing. There were questions about Jesse I couldn't answer because he never told me. He never opened himself all of the way with me. We didn't have lifelong familiarity, but I was getting closer to him every day.

The problem was that everyone felt so secure with what *they* said. *It was an accident; not a murder.* But no one knew what I knew. I experienced the missing parts to this case, and *they* only wanted to end the grieving process as quickly as they could without looking back. I knew there was something else missing.

My first question: "*Who would want to murder Jesse?*" I started with his background information.

He grew up in the American suburbia lifestyle. He lived an ordinary southern life. One that was normal and boring. He wasn't a risk taker. He usually chose the safe way of doing everything, and I tried to moderate that weak part of his personality. In my selfishness, he died.

He was a kid that everyone would jeer because it was easy. He was a simple target, an annoying, parent-approving rule follower. He would be the one kid who told the truth too much. He was especially interested in knowing things about other people. He thought if he knew people before they got a chance to know him, he would have an advantage in the conversation. By finding their interest, he could manufacture a connection with them. He wanted them to see he had something they could like about him too. He had that standard for everyone he met. *He drove on one of those safe roads less traveled by others, one that avoided conflict at all costs.*

Jesse was obsessed with pleasing and helping people. If he wasn't helping people somehow or in some way, he was thinking about a way to help someone. It sounds exaggerated, but Jesse had a heart of a giant. He only wanted to see people happy. That's why Jesse wanted to become a teacher. A teacher can impact a kid, changing that child's whole life. He wanted to have that type of effect on his students. He loved people; he was a true twenty-first century philanthropist.

I only knew pieces of Jesse. He only let people he barely knew, like me, know certain things about him. To Jesse, people wanted the surface but not the scars. He could give them facts about his life, but the details were kept inside. He wasn't asking them for help, and he did not want them to feel compelled to put their energy into him. He did not want to appear weak, unable to take care of himself. Jesse learned this behavior of self-reliance by observing the weaknesses of others.

I tried using my knowledge of psychology to analyze his behavior. I noticed that he seemed to be hiding something from everyone. He portrayed a perfect image of the happiest man on earth, but I felt like there was something slowly eating Jesse. Something didn't feel right with him, but I could never ask what was bothering him.

It was almost like I was scared to ask him, because he was such a valuable friend to me. By prying, I thought I might lose him. I suggested to myself that the volatility of our relationship was self-prescribed. He never did anything to make me feel like he would ditch out on our friendship. He only represented a person that had something missing, and I wasn't trying to lose his trust by asking about my concerns. Jesse was too valuable to everyone for *them* to not look into his death as a murder.

Jesse seemed like he was lost about certain things, especially women. He never really asked a girl out or even approached a woman on his own. Someone always introduced him to different acquaintances. I guess you could say he didn't have a lot of practice breaking the ice with the opposite sex. If he was around someone he knew, then he became the outgoing person only his true friends knew. He started conversations and became extroverted in a matter of seconds. It was almost like meeting a new girl was too much of a risk.

He had a way of finding anything too dangerous, especially surprises. He never liked surprises. He always had a plan. He had a plan for a plan that was a backup plan for another plan that might falter. *Only if he would have known what was going to happen that night. Why did he listen to me? We should have known they were going to catch us.*

Jesse was easily driven by statements from the people he knew best. In the short year that I knew him he never participated in too many unplanned things. He liked his safe and secure life. That night changed everything, when he dropped all his insecurities about an unmapped decision that led to his murder.

To the people Jesse knew, he was just a people pleaser, constantly doing as others asked. Whether it was his girlfriend, his boys, or his parents, it didn't matter. He wanted to make them happy, especially his parents. I was astounded by his obedience. He did whatever they told him. He thought they knew what was best for him.

Jesse was like the way we view a perfect world. The perfect world that he wanted would have been built with the overwhelming honesty and trust for others he displayed to all of us. He always told the truth. Jesse was a miracle that this world did not get to witness because of an unnecessary punishment, a punishment that left him breathless. He trusted people too much.

Chapter 5

IN COLLEGE, HIS life changed for the better. Jesse had a clean slate. He left all the people who picked on him in high school. In the messed-up world of high school, people don't like people who run their life off of the fuel of honesty and truth. We are all corrupt at some point in our life. Jesse was a role model of what we all wanted to be. He was a good man, a better teacher, with the best outlook on living, and we crucified him.

He had a fresh start. I know because I was exactly the same way. In college, you are given the wonderful opportunity to create another human being in the skin you have been wearing. For Jesse, this was a gift because he made true friends. He was an open book to those closest to him. Once you were in his life, you were in for good. Only his true friends knew everything about Jesse. Six of those true friends had a part in his death.

I wanted to give back the only thing I could give Jesse, which he didn't already have. I tried to give him a broader social perspective. He needed to talk to different people to grow. I used to get upset when he didn't want to go out to a social gathering with me. I wanted other people to see what I saw in Jesse. He was someone people would like if they had a chance to meet him. When I had him around I felt like a better person because I would model his honesty. When people are with someone who displays only the truth and nothing else, through the osmosis of their presence they don't want to lie. The more I was around him, I found myself striving to be more like him. What I did not realize was that he mimicked my opinion of him. He was attempting to satisfy me and others around him with every decision that he made. As much as I liked bringing him out places, he would keep his conversations casual, never revealing any deep, meaningful thoughts. I barely knew him, and I was with him a lot.

He became one of those liberals who loved everyone and wanted to save the earth from hate, just like all of his favorite professors. *It would hurt him to find things he couldn't make better. Was his optimism abused by others? Did he put too much faith into everything his professors said? Could this be the reason he's dead?* His death has something to do with him being overly trusting. I had a hunch that this was the reason.

I gathered up the background information of Jesse's life before speaking to the first of those responsible. After the funeral, the anger that had built up inside me was starting to become visible to people he once knew. I had to be careful in order to get the information I so desperately needed. They had to let me into their confessions. I had to be able to picture the terrible night and see the suspect there facilitating the end of his life. I had to be sure it was them. I had to make sure it was their fault because the way I was going to handle the unraveling truth was going to shock everyone. Their hand had to be the hand squeezing Jesse's last exhale.

Part I

ABBY AND THE FALL OF OPTIMISM

I STARTED WITH the first person on the list. Abby, his girlfriend for many years, eventually his lover in college, at the time of the murder was only his friend. I had never met Abby, so I knew he didn't date her for at least a year. The whole time I knew him, he never said anything about her. Jesse didn't say much to me though.

Abby left the states for Europe and never returned. I called her for information about where she was living. She told me that she enjoyed her life in Europe. She was thousands of miles away. There wasn't much she could have done to facilitate or prevent his murder, but that wasn't going to stop me from interrogating her like every other suspect on the list.

Chapter 6

I WAS GOING to ride on a plane for fifteen hours. I reviled planes. I had a list of reasons why I hated planes. I know I shared some common reasons with others as well. Since the terrorist attacks in New York, the airports had changed policies. Military sergeants carrying assault rifles flooded the entry gates. The process of screening each person heightened with both attacks. I knew they were there for our own safety, but they looked so arrogant. I sensed that they were trying to make us inferior to their ranks. They were portraying themselves as a higher class, and I was never good at handling respect issues. *But who am I to judge? I would never die for a country. I would never follow a leader into the valley of death. I would never die for anything that had only the singular purpose of protecting a nation. I would die for Jesse.*

My list started with my arrival to the airport. Even if you take away all of the upscale security, the airport still had its design flaws. The airport smelled a different way than anything I had ever smelled before. It had the stench of a doctor's office mixed with New York in the morning after a major holiday. Both mixtures I loathed from my childhood.

People had to walk through a zigzagged, taped-off line down a hallway to the terminal. I never enjoyed not being able to walk straight to my destination. Twists and turns seemed pointless to me. Once you got to your airline terminal, you had to pay for your bags to be put on the plane. Then you walked further down as they checked pockets, wallets, belts, and even the shoes, as if the passenger were some kind of terrorist maniac because he had a beard. I did hear someone say that prejudice was just good cop work and in certain circumstances I'd have to agree. After the attacks, they searched everyone who was not a white American.

I like to test people, to see their restrictions. Everyone had a limit that could be pressed, and my job was to teeter on the edge of their boundaries. I wanted to see what they would do to me if I had a long beard. I was only going to be able to fulfill that dream after the case was over. If I was going to finish this, then I needed to be presentable to those people early on in my case. I needed to look the part for them to let me in on the truth of Jesse's murder. I needed to feel, sound, and especially look professional to these people.

For them to explain their innocence, I had to fit into the comfortable environment they were used to. Everyone I interrogated, all of them, were on the list. No matter what I knew or heard about them, everyone was guilty. I already proved this case was a murder in my head, but I was only a small flame to a water-hosed house, built by doubt. I had to find my own fuel because no one believed me.

I had a particular set of skills I mastered in college. I had the ability to use every one of my senses, to cipher the truth. My premeditated plan before each suspect was clear. I was skilled in nonverbal communication. I could read their face like a polygraph machine. Everyone has their own way of making the needles jump up and down. I just had to see the truth come out of them. Once I had that information, the needles on their face would supply me with the truth. I knew all of the signs of lying. The way each muscle moved in their face described a thousand words that they didn't know they gave me. My goal was to put them in a place where they could feel safe and tell me the truth. The safety I had was a guarantee that they would pay. The only way this could happen was for me to become him.

I became Jesse. Jesse was the polygraph reader. He was the friend who could make the most dishonest, unstructured asshole into the goddamn Pope. He was the key to the world becoming a better place. He was the pain of loss. His life was like a knife to my chest. I wore his mask. I became his legend.

Chapter 7

I PASSED BY the uniform looking down at the ground, without saying a word or thinking about having any other expression than business. I had to lighten up my mood in public. Jesse was harder to read than I was right then. I looked so upset and startled. My ability to hide everything had not reached its full potential.

When I looked at the guard, I started to think about work. I thought about the meaning of having a particular job. To me, every job was the duty of completing a task. A task whose only purpose was to prevent chaos. The more threat of chaos, the more that person was paid for doing their job. Someone had to do it. It was not right for me to dishonor the airport security. They were only doing their job. *It could not be a part of their benefits package to bring home the odor of the airport with them every night. You couldn't pay me enough to smell like that every day.*

Working here would be a disaster, especially after that guy flew the plane into the mosque that used to sit on ground zero. Since that event, our society had become vengeful.

One man, exactly ten years on September 11th, 2011, goes on a suicide mission flying a plane. He was alone. He flew straight into the mosque, the one that caused so much controversy when it was built over the broken foundation of the World Trade Center. Compared to the first attacks, this barely made the news. I could only question what was happening in the government and our nation. I didn't have the answers, and *they* didn't give us any either.

Jesse knew more than I did about the world and the economy. I knew it wasn't looking good. Jesse tried to tell me about how volatile the government's money was going to be in the future. He knew so much about all of those things, like social security failing, and I wished I knew half of the crap he understood. He tried to teach me, but I didn't give him the time of day. I regret that I did not take advantage of the short time I had with him. There were so many qualities I wanted to take from him.

Jesse was a sponge. He was very impressionable, like a ten-year-old boy. Unlike the typical ten-year-old boy who soaks up all of the information he can about sex and curse words, Jesse wanted to know how to do the right thing. *Anything* said from *anyone* he trusted was the right thing.

The hallway fell into a slant. I watched as people leaned back to balance out the angle in which we were walking. The plane was extremely small and not to my liking. The doorway to the plane was made for people smaller than six feet. I had to duck my way into the cabin.

Something positive—the flight attendant was stunning. Her body was shaped like a thin hourglass. Her clothes were professional, and they were skin tight on her curves. She was in her mid-thirties and beautifully put together. High cheekbones complimented her facial structure. I would have thought she loved her job because she seemed happy when she greeted each person onto the plane with, "Hello. How are you?" She smiled big and looked each person in the eye, but what gave her away was the early release of her upper cheek muscles after she gave each ticketholder a brief grin. She looked as if she wanted people to see that she wasn't really smiling. *Was there a terrorist on the plane? Was this a sign?* Breathing hard and feeling totally ridiculous, I convinced myself to think about something else.

"Are you okay?" She put her arm on me, feeling my discomfort of riding on planes.

"Sorry. I was just thinking about something."

"No problem. Would you like a complimentary brown bag?" I started to grin and contemplated accepting her donation.

"No. That hasn't happened in years."

With both of us laughing, I could still hear the mumble of upset passengers behind us. The faint comment of a man behind sounded like, "Come on man, get her number and move on."

I hesitantly boarded the plane, which smelled more like vinegar and unmasked body odor. I was too anxious to care about the stench. I disliked nothing more than planes. Even the people working on the planes had something to do with my fear of aircrafts. They were ruthless in their humor. Once I had a lady tell me, "Since we have very few passengers on this plane, we will have to even out the weight."

Are you kidding me? Even out the weight? What the hell is that supposed to mean? Couldn't she just say move to the back of the plane? Our ignorance would hide the truth of our flight safety. That's what the government does every day.

"Move toward the back to prevent us from doing a nose dive onto the landing area."

This obnoxious woman was laughing as she said those discomforting words. It was this kind of comment that made me go crazy. I don't remember exactly what I said to her after she made the joke, but I remember that USA Airway Express advised me not to use joining flights through them anymore.

I admit that I was letting those little things ruin my trip. The honest truth about airports, airport security, and planes is that all of this loathing comes from one repeated occurrence. It's the feeling of buoyancy after lifting off the ground. I don't know how else to describe the feeling other than comparing it to a roller coaster that has reached the top. There is that brief moment where the car has stopped moving up, then brief but inevitable weightlessness. This was the same sensation I got when the plane leveled out. All passengers on the airplane are leaning back, but not like walking down the terminal hallway. It's a forced pressure given by the aircraft rather than a balancing. Finally, the pressure lifts its hands off the passengers as the plane surpasses the five-thousand-foot altitude. That leveling out feeling seemed more like a minor plunge.

People over-justify the fact that there are more people who die in cars than in airplanes. That might be true, but I'll be damned if I don't like the fact I have a chance to live after a car wreck, when my car breaks down, or when money becomes so tight that I run out of gas. The bad economy had taken such an enormous toll on people's lives, it made me wonder about the air carrier's position. Money was not readily available anymore, and there was no bailout money left from the government. Not only was I concerned about the likelihood of the plane stalling and falling in mid-flight, I also contemplated the chance the airline might not have adequate funding for fuel. I'm pretty certain if you run out of money to fuel a plane; there isn't even a slight chance of surviving.

I had to stop thinking about those awful, improbable scenes in my head. I abhorred lying so much that I forced myself to delete my thoughts about the rest of that dreadful flight.

Chapter 8

I TRAVELED TO Spain for this investigation. I was going to find out what everyone else had refused to admit. I needed to know more. *How was she involved? Who were his assailants?* I had to know why she was on the list. There was a reason she was called. I had to find out why, and using the money I saved up from graduation was worth every penny to find the answers. This was the first time I sent thank-you letters out for gifts from relatives and family friends.

All of the airports I have been to in my life seem to be designed by the same blueprint. Everything was the same. I had to go through Spanish Customs to get my bags checked again. As I walked up to the foreign speaking native, I knew this was going to take longer than I wanted. He spoke to me in Spanish. As he spoke his voice began to rise. Although I did not understand him, it was evident he was upset. I understood the emotion in his voice, but not a single hour of Spanish One or Spanish Two helped me comprehend a word he said.

His eyebrows gave me a clue. When his eyebrows were perched up and his eyelids opened, he was asking a question. I needed to find out what objects of mine he was interested in. Obviously, I did not respond to his demands fast enough because his head tilted downward and eyebrows fell to a strain. He was angry that I could not understand even the hand motions he gave me.

After ten minutes of staring and understanding nothing from this guy, he searched my bag and asked for my passport. I bought this passport just for this trip. I had never been outside of the United States. The only reason I felt the need to fly over here was to talk to her. She had to give me something worth taking home.

I finally made it upstairs and out of the front doors. I was amazed at how this place looked. The speed of everything seemed faster than in Greensboro, NC. They walked with conviction; like they had a place to be with only seconds to spare. This place was at my kind of pace.

I walked to the first street corner and took a look at my map. I knew she did not live too far away so I just had to find the names of two consecutive streets to see where I was on the map.

Spain was set up in a very peculiar way in comparison to home. The design was convenient and the society here was full of culture and tradition. Luckily, Spain had a grid system, but not in the way you would picture if you have ever been to New York. The grid wasn't in square blocks like Manhattan. It seemed like every street curved a new way.

I had heard some great things about this place. They drink all night and sleep all day. It looked like every single one of my college habits in one country. I noticed people seemed happy. They all had a purpose, a reason to move the way they did. They had a place to be, but they did not allow themselves to feel hurried. I had a destination as well. My motivation was to refute the current idea everyone had about Jesse's death and prove my case. I wanted to lose this heavy burden I carried with me. To add to the weight I had been carrying since he died, I felt like gathering information was going to need further validity.

My complexion stuck out in the crowd. I was pale and looked like I had not slept in days. Everyone had a wonderful skin complexion. They looked as perfect as brown could look. Their skins glistened in the sun.

I couldn't understand why these people were so damn happy. *Was it making me angry that people were happy or was I angry that I wasn't happy like them? What's wrong with me?*

The only drawback to living in this wonderful place would be the cultural differences. I would have to learn a whole new language, develop the skill for reading people's nonverbal communication, and dress like a total Guido. I was lost in the sound of separation here. I just graduated with a degree in communication and psychology. In six years of college, I didn't learn anything about communication in places outside the U.S.

It was like Jesse said, "College is all theory and not enough practical application. These professors work with their head in the clouds while we work in the trenches where it is real."

I missed him.

"Excuse me, miss?" I was hoping for success and not yet another failed attempt at communication.

"Yes, you are not from here, correct?" Her accent was to die for. I started to think with juvenile tendencies about what I wanted do to her. *I imagined how the fine act of two backs and no face would feel.*

I had to remember why I was here. Nothing could come in between me and solving this case.

"Yes, I am looking for 41 Escuintla?"

"Here, take this," she said as she handed me her map. "I have been here so long that I will not need it any longer."

She could tell I was still lost. She knew that if she just gave me the map and walked away, it wouldn't help. She put her index and middle finger on a street corner and turned her shoulders back to me.

"This is where we are standing right now."

"Thank you very much."

I contemplated whether this woman might be Abby, but she would have noticed the address that I said I was trying to find. I shrugged it off and headed west to the next street corner.

I was only twenty-two blocks away.

Jesse didn't tell me too much about her, but like the rest of people on the list, he didn't have to tell me too much. *It always came to me.* "When we have our back against the wall and there is nothing to do but succeed, then that's when we do everything we can to make sure success becomes the only outcome of our efforts." Even with *them* breaking the door down, I was going to succeed. I had nothing left. No reason to carry on with anything else until I found Jesse's murderer.

She opened the door and waved me into the hut. This wasn't like the houses we had in the United States, but it was exactly the same as every other house in the neighborhood's proximity. *Was she running away from something back there?*

Abby was a very beautiful girl. He must have been with her after he grew into his attractive days. Jesse, like most people, went through an awkward phase. The phase where you start to grow into an older looking person, but still have reminisces of your adolescence. I only know because of high school pictures. In college, he grew out of it and started to look older. He grew taller, and his facial hair helped him with the transitioning phase of teenage to adulthood.

She lived in a house with other people who only spoke Spanish. It appeared she was teaching them how to speak English and vice versa. Abby must have been a Spanish major. I imagined her goal might have been to get a translation job in Spain. When I entered the house with Abby to talk to her, I noticed she had grown accustomed to the Spanish culture. She wore a thin dress with a Jerry Garcia, trippy design down to her ankles. She must have had her hair darkened, and she was as tan as everyone else in Spain. The curls in her hair suggested that she might have Spanish heritage.

She must have never eaten meat a day in her life because her figure was something out of the ordinary.

As people we adapt to fit in to certain surroundings even when we try our best to keep ourselves true to our idea of individuality. I'm not saying Abby changed for the worse, nor did she purposely make herself fit in; it is just an innate adaptation. I didn't know much about Abby, so I was a little ambiguous when it came to their break up. *Had Abby moved away to Europe to go away from Jesse? Had Jesse driven her away?*

Chapter 9

THROUGH MY LONG thought process of assumptions and predictions, there was an awkward silence. In the silence I keep to myself and think about the situation and take in all of the factors. It might freak people out because while I do this my eyes roll back in my head and I do not say a word. Ever since that fatal night, I have to cut into everything to make sure I don't miss any important leads to this case.

"Hello Abby." I slowly started to make out the shadow shapes in front of my blurring vision.

"Are you okay? You passed out standing up for a minute."

I probably needed to sit down. But I knew this was natural for me to do this. The worst thing about my new habit was that everyone asked the same question every time. Like Jesse, I tried not to make it obvious to others, especially since this whole thing was for him.

I had to go directly to the business part of this interrogation.

"I remember giving you a call to talk to you about Jesse's life up until his death."

I saw her emotions fade from concern of my health to the heartache she must of felt. *Did she lose a friend or a lover? It was too soon to tell, but I recognized the pain in her eyes.*

"I don't have that much to tell you about his life in the past two years D ..."

I cut her off before she could say it.

"How about we skip the whole name thing?"

I was no longer the person I was before. I had to become Jesse if I was going to solve this mystery, because these people were the only ones allowed into Jesse's comfort zone. Without comfort, I would only obtain lies and manipulative bending of the truth. Jesse was all truth, and these people absorbed that trait from him when he was alive. I had to become everything Jesse created to be able to see this case through to the end. To be him, I had to walk like him, talk like him, act like him, and I had to feel like him. Jesse's blood was my blood.

"Okay Jesse. Like I was saying, I have lived here for years now, and I don't know if I will be of much help to your investigation."

I could see she had a good heart because she seemed to feel sorry for me flying all of the way to Spain when she was most likely not immediately useful for me or Jesse's mystery. But that was her just being nice.

She was very easy going, perfect for Jesse. Abby was a modern day hippie who would have been nice to even the people who say the most terrible things about her. Just like Jesse.

Chapter 10

"JUST TELL ME something unique about Jesse. Like if I really …" I exaggerated the length of the word, "knew Jesse, I would know …"

I gave her a hand motion to let her know that I wanted her to finish my sentence. Abby's patience and general concern for a stranger like me was a quality of hers that I came to admire.

"Well, Jesse was my boyfriend in college, and we had known each other for, like, years."

How did she know that I wouldn't know about them?

"We basically grew up together. Jesse had a different breed of personality than I was used to in a boyfriend. I had known him almost my whole life."

I saw the muscles in her face wanting to display a smile about memorable times with her significant other; but she hid them like they weren't supposed to be there. I wanted to learn more about their relationship with every pause she gave me.

Her pauses allowed me time to think about how all relationships are learning experiences and are truly a required part of life. I remember in college we studied about how many crazy people there were in the world. *The ones who didn't have anyone to tell them they loved them. I bet if someone told Charles Manson he was loved, he wouldn't have been so crazy.* Probably not. *Maybe his followers were crazy people who never had a true love relationship? That's why they were followers with no hesitation. Maybe he told them he loved them. Maybe that's why people join gangs? They don't have the parental love that they need and receive love from others with the same pain.* It's when we can relate that we open up. And opening up was what I needed from her.

With a picture perfect image of the filthy Charles Manson, I had to find another comparison to love. To me, love is a crazy vehicle to people with no experience. If someone has never driven it before and their feet are either too sensitive or too abrupt on the pedals, they will never find the right medium to start driving the car. Once the car starts moving, one way or another, it's like driving with two feet. One person has the upper hand; they are the brake. It doesn't take much energy for the brakes to work. These kinds of people are in control. They can let the car drive by easing off the brakes, or they can slam down those brakes any time they want; brakes always beat the gas pedal. The other person, who wants the car to drive, puts all of their weight down on the gas pedal. If the brakes are being pushed down at the same time, these people are wasting all of their pathetic energy into making something work that inevitably will never happen. Instead of increasing the distance of love, they keep the wheels spinning in one place until the tires blow. And all that really matters in the end is that you loved.

I wonder if this was Jesse's first relationship where there was mutual affection, not a codependent one. They probably kept their regular routines, maintained their daily lives and kept their friends, which had become uncommon these days. This relationship was true love. I can tell all of this by the way she carried herself. *The way she talked. The way she told her stories. She was confident. She did not need to have someone. That's why Jesse loved her.*

Chapter 11

WE SAT ON the big couch in the living room. I didn't remember sitting down or walking through the door. I felt like I did when I woke up in a bed that was not my own. I quickly scanned the furniture in the room and gathered a list of possibilities about how I got here.

"Are you okay?" Abby started to look at my wound, and she tried to take care of me. "You are bleeding, and you kind of looked like you dozed off for a second. What happened?"

I wanted to say something that would make her understand why I did this to myself. *None of them would understand, only Jesse.* I had to think and get myself in the right state of mind for solving this mystery.

She grabbed a napkin and said, "Here, put this on the wound and sit down."

I wanted to say I was sorry for bleeding on her floor, but instead I got back to business. "Why do you think Jesse died?"

She dropped the napkin like I was the mailman after a war, bringing the notarized letter to widows who just found their new life without a passenger in the car. She started to tremble, reluctantly holding back her tears.

"Well, uh. Jesse … always depended on himself to get through tough situations, and I think in a lot of his situations, he needed someone to hear him out. He needed someone to help him through the hard times. He had no one to help him through that rough patch in his life."

I could understand her logic. She was right. Whenever I needed someone to vent, my mother was always my best listener.

"So do you think Jesse was fatalistic? I mean he could have tried to get out of it."

This question was almost a rhetorical question to me now. I was already used to people telling me that he wasn't, so they felt like they could keep his pride for him. Stupid people. His pride can neither be damaged nor replaced, and what happened can never be changed. *Forever can't be changed.* I just needed to find out how and why to make my judgment clear. *I understood why she thought she was doing a noble act for the dead by how she embraced the good in him and how he changed her life.* Remembering the bad is like the bitter truth that we try to avoid at all costs.

"No … he was full of life."

"But didn't he think about death at all, when those toughest of hard times piled up on him?"

I knew that she was going to bring retaliation for the need to keep his pride gold. But that was an illusion of safety; it wasn't going to help.

"Yes he did, but …"

"But I already know how great of a person he was, and he did a lot to make this world better. For instance, he was the leader in raising money for the swimming club. He volunteered more time in the week than he worked. He was always finding a reason to think his life was worth living. He found the safety of life through other people's happiness; anyone who was happy, whether Jesse was responsible for their emotion or not, he joined them in their happiness. He cared for people. I need you to tell me something about him that I don't already know."

As she was about to speak I could see it on her face, an accrued sense of animosity towards my comments, and I knew she was about to question why I was here. *It's not always what you say but how you say it.*

"If you already knew all of that, then why are you here?" That became proof. I could make even the nicest person I ever met angry.

"Abby there is no need to get upset about my curiosity. I just want the cold and seemingly terrible truth about my friend." I was giving her a sympathetic look in an attempt to reach past her anger at my questions.

"Okay. I didn't know it was going to be this hard to talk about Jesse. I could tell you all these great things about Jesse …" She quickly recovered from that statement as she saw my mouth beginning to open as if I was going to interrupt her." … but you already know that about him." My face said thank you with a head nod and a fake grin.

Chapter 12

"You're right. Jesse had a fatalistic personality hidden behind his overall love for the world."

Now, I was getting what I needed. I needed the truth of Jesse. I needed the secrets he kept locked away.

"He wouldn't let little things bother him in the present, but they just kept bottling up. My guess is that he had no one to talk to about that pain he suffered that night."

This was one assumption by my suspect that I knew the answer to already, firsthand.

"He needed someone to be there for him, and no one was there."

She started to stutter while her shallow breath became weaker. She sat up and moved to the love chair, which was closer to the tissues.

Before I could say anything to keep her going, she said, "Jesse changed when he came to college. He became more confident, and with his confidence he gained many more insecurities than he ever had before. He needed someone that night, and no one was there for him. Maybe that's why …"

"We are still in the process of finding the truth of his death."

"Illek had to be the one."

"What?" I hadn't spent enough time with her to make a final analysis. I was never sober when I met Illek and neither was she. I made a promise to myself at the first establishment of this case. I wrote down that, "I would not let the perception of anyone on the list alter my perception of someone else on the list," but I trusted her opinion. Abby's presence was undemanding.

"I understand it now. Something happened between him and Illek that night. She probably went on one of her temper rages and drove him off the edge."

"Please go on. Are you sure of this?" My eyes were more purposeful than a lion seeking a meal after three weeks of hunger. *Was she claiming one of my priority suspects as the killer?*

"Not exactly sure, it was just a gut feeling."

Even though I was disappointed she did not know the full truth, her persona was the reason I let her continue. "I mean, I came home to see my parents in Maryland, back in December. I really wanted to see Jesse, too. I was thinking of moving back home. I wanted it to be a surprise for him that I was coming back for good."

I understood what that meant. She was going to come back for him.

"So Illek and Jesse were in a relationship, and he couldn't come to see you?" My skills were progressing as this case moved along.

"Sort of … he said they were on a break. I came down to North Carolina to see him. It was just supposed to be him and me, like always. We were supposed to have dinner. I was going to tell him I was ready."

"He had someone with him, and you never told him." I felt like I should have followed the arrogance of my premonition with a bow.

"Yes." She became saddened with the news she was about to give me, and I knew I had to pull this information out of her gently.

Chapter 13

"SHE WASN'T SUPPOSED to be there. She was supposed to be angry at him for something, anything. My timing was all wrong. She found out I was coming into town, and she clawed her hooks on him tighter and tighter so there was no chance of losing him to me."

"Why did you move? Was it because of Jesse?"

She got up from the love chair and walked to the kitchen. "No."

Once again she paused. She pulled out the coffee pot that scented the room with a vanilla caramel aroma. Pouring coffee into a mug, Abby seemed to want to say something but hesitated. She took one sip from her cup and closed her eyes before she said, "I moved because I had already planned this move, months before I fell in love with him. I wasn't supposed to fall in love with him. He wanted me to stay, and he told me he loved me. I was scared, and I didn't know what to do. I had my mind set and my future planned."

"Didn't you love him?"

"Yes … but at the time I was already committed to the translation program. I had a job to do here."

"If you love someone there are no boundaries to that love. Why didn't you keep the relationship after you moved here?"

Even from afar your vehicle can have the equal pressing and giving of the pedals; there's just a time delay.

"He wanted to do that, and I knew he would stay faithful to me ... that was never a problem between us. He knew nothing but certainties, sincerity, and loyalty. It would have worked out if we tried."

"But?"

"I told him I didn't know when I was coming back, and he shouldn't put his life on pause for me. I thought he would respond ... I thought he would say he would wait for me, but he didn't. He said, "I love you and good-bye." She tried to blame Jesse partially for her leaving.

Chapter 14

THERE WAS A long pause. She came back into the living area and sat back down in the love chair. I didn't know what to say or how to say it. Then she spoke again.

"I bought a one-way ticket home. We were going to start where we left off. We were going to fall back in love and share stories about what we had done all these years. But she was there and he would never know. She didn't deserve him. She was using him to better herself. She was so pessimistic and he was so optimistic. He was way too good for her. He was still in love with me."

She looked down and pointed to her chest. "I could tell. It was in his eyes. He wanted us to work out again, but he was trapped. He had too much respect for me, himself, and for … her." The last three letters of that statement were spoken with so much disgust that I actually considered that she had at least one hateful bone in her body. *She hated Illek.*

"So you moved back here?"

"The end. The story of my life."

She smacked her thighs and looked up to the ceiling, like her own hopeful personality became tainted with cynical infection.

"Now I can't feel anything, for anyone, from anyone, or at least not like I did for Jesse. There are people in this world who are fated for each other, and that was the two of us."

This statement about fate agitated me. *I was no one's puppet. I made my own fate. This was my self-created destiny. I knew where and when I was going. No one else had it planned out for me. I was my own God.* She said one word, 'fated', that capsized my buoyant boat into a sea of anger, and I couldn't listen to her anymore. I was ready to analyze her reaction to the truth of why I was here.

I hated fate. My faith was a bible soaked in grease, and Jesse's death was the fire. No wind or holy water could stop my faith from burning. When people spoke of or pushed faith on me, my fire got stronger. No one had what was needed to put out my fire.

Chapter 15

"Thank you, Abby. You have been such a lovely suspect."

She paused. The term "suspect" had triggered something unpredictable. I never expected her, of all people, to react as she did.

"Suspect?" she yelled. "What the hell are you talking about?"

Yes, bring me this truth. What do you think of me? Show me your anger. Show me the truth in your pain, and you will be set free of my investigation.

"Are you even a paid investigator? Let me see some kind of identification. This has been completely ridiculous! You can't just come into my house and think you own my life. My God, it's like you already knew all of this stuff about Jesse and just wanted to hear it come from someone else's mouth. What are you doing here?"

I was in no mood to answer disobliging questions.

"I can tell you that you are doing more damage to me, and yourself, by conducting this so-called investigation."

That may be true, but when the final curtain falls, pain *will be the reason this case ends.*

"It's not even a murder, you asshole. We all know what happened. Please leave. Can't you tell that I am uncomfortable with this conversation?" *She was talking as if death was supposed to be*

51

something people could talk about over coffee.

"Please leave. Leave now."

"I have all the information I need from this conversation. I know it's hard to cope with forever. Forever is only accomplished by an ugly truth that rears its head when there's no other choice. Abby, have a wonderful life and peace be with you." I was speaking over the shuffling noises caused by her trying to push me out of the doorway.

Her anger was immediate, caused by one simple word, reminding her of the exact reason she moved away from Jesse. It was almost humorous to see how grief could turn into rage in the split second of saying one misplaced word. *Suspect.*

Happiness can be manipulated by a series of misplaced words and takes longer to switch to anger. Unhappiness and anger are so close to the same emotion, sometimes I confused it for one and the same.

I opened the door to leave, looked back and then spoke. "You should understand that I know he called you that night."

I finished the look I gave her after saying what I needed to say. Then I heard a whisper from her weeping face. She was attempting to say, "Get out."

She was on the list, and she spoke about another suspect on the list. I needed to meet Abby for the simple reason of knowing all the suspects on the list. I know it broke my initial rule about this investigation, but her personality seemed to be the closest to Jesse's I'd ever seen. I came here to Spain because I needed a jump start. I needed to know the order of justice I was going to bring to them. She was far down the list. She couldn't have told *them* to kill Jesse, but she could still help me with other suspects. I thought, '*I have to stay here, at least for one more day.*'

I couldn't go back to see her yet. I had to wait until she cooled off. She wasn't going to be able to help me with the strong hatred she had for me right now.

Chapter 16

"Hey Mom, I was just about to call you."

"I told you to call me when you got settled in." I could almost see her pointing her finger at me from an ocean away.

"I know. I had to take care of the business part of my trip, and now I'm almost settled." She knew some of what I was doing with Jesse's death. I told her I was making a bigger collection of memories.

"Well, I was worried about you, so I called a hotel. They have an English translator through the concierge department. I got a room for you. The reservation is open-ended so you can stay as long as you want. I know you want to see the beaches down there." Her kind voice made me feel bad about not staying there.

"Thanks. You didn't have to do that, Mom."

"I know, but I figured it could be part of your graduation present."

Laughing, I realized that I'm very lucky to have a mother like her. I could tell her everything … Well, almost everything. I couldn't tell her that I wasn't going to use the hotel because she would worry about where I was sleeping. I had my own plan. *Jesse always had a plan.*

"It took me long enough, didn't it?"

With a giggle from her I knew I made her feel secure. I haven't been myself since everything happened. It seemed like everyone else had moved on but me. My mom wanted me to take a vacation. They thought I needed this trip. Little did they know about how much I needed this. It wasn't a vacation to me though. I would be working, and I wasn't going to stay long. I needed to get the truth and get back to the states so I could amass all of the information from the responsible.

"At least you finished … no matter how long it took you. I'm very pro—"

"I know, Mom. Thanks for the room. I love you."

Click.

Chapter 17

A COUPLE HOURS passed, and I felt positive that Abby was calmer now. I started to draw up my conversation points with her. I had planned to ignore everything the suspects said about other suspects, but after she spoke about Illek I changed my mind. I needed to know more about his mom, Illek, and anything else she could tell me. I needed everything she could give me.

The cost of the trip was never a factor in the importance of its success. I have never cared about money. I wanted to make this trip worth it because Jesse would have. To solve this murder I had to emulate all of the values of Jesse. Life is what we habitually do. Therefore, my lifestyle, habits, and conversations with people were a mirror of who Jesse was to the people he loved.

Every day since I saw the murder scene, I have wanted to know more about Jesse. I wanted to know the way he was wired because he wasn't like the rest of us. He was a gift to anyone around him.

I walked past the downtown area. I wasn't going to go to the beaches because going there would require me to forget why I was there. I couldn't even enjoy the scenery around me. I walked up her doorstep again.

I went to knock on the side window when one of the tenants

opened the door. She allowed me to come in even though she probably heard us arguing before. She didn't even try to speak to me when I said, "Hello."

Abby was walking down the stairs; she spoke in Spanish to the tenant, and silence filled the room. I got the message she was sending. I know I had to apologize; even though I hated to ask for forgiveness. Especially when I was apologizing for something that I didn't feel was wrong. This was a very hard part of this job; lying in hopes of making suspects feel comfortable enough to spill their guts, as my self-importance slowly perished. Apologies are ways to voice regret. I never regretted anything because I always acted with purpose; with a plan. I had to swallow my pride for the sake of saving this case. I had to swallow my pride to prove that *they* were wrong.

"Abby, look …"

"Save it. I understand that you and I have both gone through a lot since his death."

I started to feel very attracted to her. She didn't change clothes or even the way her hair was from our first meeting, but she understood now. She understood what I was doing here. She didn't even allow me to apologize for the way I handled our previous conversation. She knew I needed the truth, and that was my only objective.

"Thank you."

"So tell me, why are you here again?"

Her face showed me that it was all right to be here, I only needed a good excuse. I had one too; I had just written one on paper a few moments before I came to her door. I wanted her to tell me anything she could about anyone who could have hurt Jesse that night.

"You were going to tell me something about his mother, and I cut you off before." I looked down, hoping she would see the softer side of my rough exterior.

"Well, it's not just his mother; his father wasn't really present in his life either. He worked a lot on weekdays and weekends. In high school, Jesse would religiously remind me that his father would be getting a promotion soon. He really wanted him to get that promotion. It meant no more weekends and a three hundred percent raise. Years passed and he never got that promotion. Jesse kept the naïve optimism of a four-year-old playing basketball, looking at a Michael Jordan poster." I was impressed with her knowledge of sports and the mention of a cornerstone of the NBA. I could see many qualities that made her lovable.

"So is that wh—"

"Speaking of basketball, Jesse played basketball all four years of high school."

I would normally be upset at someone interrupting me, but once again I made an exception. I think it had to do with her calming down and wanting to give me valuable information.

"I know he was still pretty good when I played him."

"Well ... kind of."

"Kind of what?"

"He kind of played all four years. See, he had Coach Smith for his freshman through junior year of basketball. Then Coach Shoemaker came in from a private school."

I could tell by her tone that this guess was going to be right. "So he was benched from playing when the new coach took over the position?"

"Worse. Coach Smith got really sick and had to stop coaching midway through the tryouts. Jesse had always made the team each year but never played over ten minutes a game. I went to every one of his games. When Coach Shoemaker took over, he did the final cuts for the team. I swear if he could have only seen how good of a player and even better of a role model he was, then Jesse would have definitely made the team. That was the strangest day for both of us. I could see it in his eyes. The bad thing about it was he wouldn't have seemed unusual to anyone else. Anyone else could have walked by him and not noticed a thing, but I did. I saw him torn apart from the inside. It's not like his parents would even notice if he made the team or not; they never came to a single game."

"That's terrible. What did you do to help him?"

I wanted to know the things I could have done differently. I know it was too late now, but I desperately desired to understand how to reach out to him. *Maybe something would have changed that night?*

"I was just there for him. I wanted him to know that I was there to talk to." She spoke insecurely. I wanted to know why she was speaking without the conviction she used before.

"Did that work?"

"No, but I used one of my talents that I observed after a fight with his mom."

She paused and started to grin. *What was she grinning for? Jesse's dead!*

"He listened to everything I said to him. He did exactly what I told him to do."

I began to think she was ready to confess to something. She seemed to uncharacteristically change the conversation. Her domination of Jesse disappointed me. I waited until she finished her statement before I fished for a confession.

"He trusted me. When you gain Jesse's trust you have gained a strong influence in his life. I never used this ability on him for my own purposes."

She spoke like she was trying to change the expression on my face from tense and confused to relaxed and understanding. She wasn't going to harm Jesse. She loved him.

"So what did you tell him?"

"I told him that he should come to the game with me so he could still see his basketball friends play. I told him that it would mean a lot to me if he was my date. My God, I gave that man so many signs."

I slowly scribed the words she said in my head and then remembered how she ended it. She said something that didn't relate to the tone of the conversation. "Signs of … ?"

She cupped her hands over her knees and said, "I loved him more than just a friend. I pretended to not know how to drive a stick-shift car for a whole year. I would come by his work and bring him lunch, and all he thought I was doing was being a good friend."

I could tell she wanted to keep her smile and the laughter with which she began the sentence. She was rocking back and forth like a teenager in love. Then, the muscles in her face started to weaken as she couldn't hold the corner of her lips up any longer. Her smile became strained, and I could see her start to break down.

I sat down closer to her. Comforting her, I watched the other tenant in the house leave the room. I rubbed circular motions on her back, making her feel safe with me.

"I know this is hard."

"I never should have left. He opened up to me, and I thought I had to leave him because I didn't want my life to keep running on a treadmill. I wish I could go back and change."

I stopped comforting and began to lean backwards. We were sitting on the couch in the living room with a small hint of light coming from one of the two windows. I hated when people talked about regret. I could not stand those words because I was in self-denial that I didn't have any regret from that night. I wanted to stop thinking about what she said. I tried to swallow a gulp of new air to keep this act going. It didn't work.

"Yeah, I know you would like to go back, but you can't! No one can. We can't change what happened. So just stop this conversation at I loved him and don't talk about changing anything, because you can't."

She crawled away from me. With her tears stopping and her eyes wide opened, staring at me with fear she said, "Why are you doing this? Why did you come here to do this to me?"

"Why am I doing this? I'm doing this because no one else will. You all just accepted what happened, turned away from the truth and allowed them to take his life with no payment. They owe me, us, the payment of their lives for taking his. Do you not see what has happened here?"

"What are you saying?" Speaking tentatively, her response was very unlike her previous request for me to leave. This time she was scared of me. I'd already blown this conversation, so I thought that I might as well spill it.

"You know, I came here because I thought you were different. I thought you could help me. I got some good stuff, but I needed more from you."

She said nothing and started crying again. I started to leave, and I was hoping she would say something that would make me stay. Once again, silence filled the room, and I clearly got the message that she wanted me to leave. Although leaving this room meant I no longer had her support, I carried onward.

I stood up and thought of anything I could use to close this conversation, but the old woman came back into the room speaking Spanish. She gave me the look I needed to leave and not come back. I opened the door and took a deep breath before walking out.

Walking down the winding road to the airport, my mind was cluttered with thoughts of the investigation. I needed something to help me gain confidence again. I got what I needed from her, and I just had to accept that not every one of the suspects would give me something to write home about. I had to dig. After penning a check mark next to Abby's name, I perused the five suspects' names that I had left.

Chapter 18

Sitting down in the same terminal I came out of, I thought about my conflict with Abby. I wanted to think that I never left, that I never said good-bye, and I never called her a suspect. She supported me. She knew exactly what I was doing for Jesse and backed me up on it. *Only the ashes of burning bridges remind us that the soil on each side no longer shared a common ground.*

I had a lot of time to think. The next flight wasn't for four hours, and even then I had a connecting flight from Maryland Heights, Missouri. I knew what I had to do when I got back to the states. I had no more business in Spain. I had so much to analyze at home. The only aspect of my life that I could even fake a smile to, was Jesse. I wasn't doing this to somehow keep his pride; instead, I needed this investigation to bring the pain I felt to those responsible.

I was busy this time on the plane ride back. I did not enjoy even one second of the trip. I was doing something I said I would never do again, flying, because I needed to find the truth. I was willing to do *anything* to find it.

"First unheard message."

"Hey, I didn't like the way we ended our conversation last night.

61

Please call me back. Remember this is not your fault. So don't beat yourself up over it. I love you."

"Message erased."

"Fasten your seatbelts at this time. Please turn off all electronic devices and prepare for liftoff."

The bottle told me to take two after dinner. I had to take six to get sleep. I couldn't sleep on my own. *Hopefully I will be asleep before we lift off and level out.*

Journal Entry

It's over now, and I wish I could take it back. I will never forget her. She understands me. She was everything to me. She knew everything about me. She was there for me that night. I will never forget that because it won't leave my head. That night was like a thought you tried to tell yourself you don't want to think about; but you still do. Your mind doesn't listen to your words because words can be manipulated in partial truths and lies. Your mind is something that is always true.

I remember the night I was sixteen years old and getting my first cell phone. My parents were always trying to buy nice things for me so I would be happy. The things they gave me weren't anything special. I know I should have been grateful for getting anything from my parents. There are people in this world who wouldn't get a crumb of food from their parents. I should be thankful for their gifts, but why would they give me a cell phone for emergencies only? When I call them, they never call me back. How would they know if it was an emergency or not? Why would they not call me back? Too busy, I guess. Because of my parents, the word busy became a cancer to my heart. Were they really too busy to spend time with their own son? Were my parents too busy to love me? It seemed like any time I brought this up to them, they kind of laughed it off and gave me these meaningless gifts. I was at the age where I didn't want anything from them anymore. I was going to earn it through work.

That night I was driving in an emotional state at three in the morning to return their gift. I wrote a letter to my mother. It said terrible things about how I didn't need anything they ever gave me. I returned the phone to them because it was the last thing they gave to me. Keeping the phone was a symbol that I approved of their way of validating their neglect. I had to get rid of it.

I wasn't exactly mad at my dad because he was a stranger my whole life. I didn't even find out that my dad's lack of presence was abnormal until I met Abby's parents. They were always around, and Abby turned out great. She hadn't even left the ground yet, and I missed her.

My dad was supposed to be able to work less and get paid more, but I didn't know how he was going to manage that. My mom was theoretically a stay-at-home mom. She used to not have a job. Even though she would leave me in the car while she would go to people's houses, I still enjoyed the moments I had with her. When she got her job and I was a teenager, I lost those moments with her. I wonder if they even really wanted me. Maybe they were just waiting for me to turn eighteen and say "good luck." Through high school she was never there for me. She acted like a phone could represent her presence in my life, and she didn't feel the need to do anything else to clean up our damaged relationship.

Since I was six years old I have never cried in front of someone, but that night Abby was my witness. She listened so well. She let me sleep at her house for months. I didn't talk to my mom for months. She called once. She only called me once when I had been waiting for days upon weeks for her to call. I will never be able to hate someone, but I strongly despised her. I didn't want to reconcile with her. I barely even wanted to hear about her. She knew where I was, and she didn't come after me. I thought I could do it, you know, never speak to her again. I was becoming this angry entity instead of a living individual. I guess all I wanted was for her to accept that I wanted to be a teacher and not everything I did had to be for money. My parents kicked me out of their lives as soon as I was able to walk on my own.

I made a decision very early on in my life to not live the life they lived. They were always uptight about something costing too much, and they stressed each other out talking about debts and shopping sprees. I wanted my life to be secure but adventurous. I wanted to have a job where I could induce life-altering moments for children. It's like Dr. Ennis said, "Kids are baby goats, but we can teach children to fly." They wouldn't accept my dreams, my aspirations. My mom especially disagreed with my decision to turn down some technical engineer school for education. She never really cared for my opinion on my own life. It was like she was driving my life the way she wanted to drive her own. She was selfish that way. I remember telling myself not only was I going to run away, but I was never going to fucking speak to her again.

Abby told me something one day that changed my perspective. She said, "No matter how much you think your mother is wrong, she is still your mother. You can't erase sixteen years of your life. If you need something to remember, remember that she gave you life. Jesse, I only want to tell you this because I can see that it is eating away at you. At first I thought you started listening to new music because you wanted something new. Then I realized that you started listening to this music because they speak about the things that you have been through. I know what's going on here, and I'm worried. I have never seen you like this, Jesse. What happened to that guy, my best friend who would do anything for anyone? What happened to that guy who told me he loved me after we went to the movies for the first time together? Where is that Jesse smile?"

She was my best friend. Except this time my parents didn't take her away. She faded away on her own. I don't understand how I feel right now. I told her I loved her, and she ran away from me. I want to hate her so bad, but I can't. I still love her, and when you love someone like this you can't abandon the sensation of love and compassion with that person. I will always love Abby. She will always be the one that got away.

Part II

WHEN WE LOOK UP TO SOMEONE,
SOMETIMES WE FORGET TO SEE IF
THEY HAVE FEET.

"HOLD ON, HOLD on. Everybody quiet for a second."

I was standing on top of the table now, announcing something that Jesse would probably hate me for. I felt a need to do this for him. I was also a little inebriated. The boxed-in, tight crowd stopped what they were doing and looked up at me. I could hear mumbling around me, but I decided not to listen. Instead, I prepared a very short speech that would get the reaction of the home team scoring a touchdown.

"We've got a first timer here. Jesse has never done a keg stand. Let's …"

Before I was able to finish, Spencer and Noah from the rugby team picked him up by his legs. For a second, I regretted what I did, but I gave up on stopping them. I saw Jesse's face, and my regret faded away. Smiling and laughing, he was a trooper, never complained about anything. They carried him over the keg that was sitting on top of a bench. Jesse grabbed the handles and prepared to show off his athletic ability. Noah carried the hose and pressed down on the lever, releasing the valve that poured beer down his throat. And then the clutters of people were counting for him, "one, two, three, four, five, six, ahhh!" The room started to fill itself with the intoxicating laughter of the people in the room. Inhaling the breath of anyone in the room could have put anyone under the influence.

Jesse wasn't fighting it. He was okay with his reality, and he was upside-down on the keg longer than I have ever done before. So now I was getting grief. I had to prove my worth to Jesse. It was my first time ever out with him, and I had known him for nearly a year now.

"Come on man … a rookie's beating you bro!"

My Irish disease enjoyed the company of competition, as long as it had anything to do with ethanol. "Win or lose, we booze" was the motto of the club sports at the University of North Carolina at Greensboro. Everybody knew we were having a party after a game no matter what. That's what I loved about college. I made my friends through the four years of playing in the club sports. I wanted him to make friends like I did. *He* deserved that.

"Shut that shit up, freshman, before I kick your ass." I was always getting grief for playing soccer instead of rugby and for being a communications major with a minor in psychology. Apparently, girls and faggots were the only ones who had this major. I disagreed.

Before I approached my challenge, I noticed Jesse was receiving an earful from his girlfriend. She did not look happy. She had this disappointed look on her face. *Maybe if I talk to her, everything will be okay.* She was a little fireball. Even though she had a control issue with Jesse, I still felt the need to gain her approval. I wanted her to like me because I would be one of his best friends. I did not like her controlling personality, but who am I to say something to someone I barely knew? Besides, I felt a little responsible for what happened.

I started to hang from the grip of two barbaric men, but I couldn't focus on what was happening to me. I grabbed the handles of the keg and watched as she reamed him out more than before.

What was she saying? I felt like my relationship with her was starting off in shambles. This was the first time I saw her over an extended period of time. Every time I saw her, she was complaining about something, and she usually had a couple of her sorority friends with her. She was constantly annoyed with someone or something. There's no way she should've gotten that mad at Jesse for doing a keg stand. *What the hell was her problem? What was really going on?*

I stopped at six because beer started running down my face onto my jacket. I wanted to go over there and try to mend this broken situation, but then she left. *What was her name again?* She left and slammed the door hard enough to silence the no-neck barbarians in the room for a full second. *I knew what was going to happen now. Why did Jesse always crawl back to her?*

Chapter 19

SUPPORTING THE IDEA of his continuous need to please were his relationships with the professors on campus. It's like they say, "If you're not a democrat in college, you have no heart. If you are not a republican by the time you're fifty, you have no brain." Jesse always followed his professor's work and ideologies. He enjoyed being in the presence of good teachers. It's like when you want to become an aspiring author, you go to a library and fill your surroundings with the words from famous authors. He surrounded himself with the people he wanted to become.

I don't understand why this person was on the list. *Why would he call her?* I wondered about it constantly. His relationship with this teacher was much more of a wreck than anything else. I remember hearing so many things about this professor that would make me think that there was something I was missing. *Had their relationship changed? Was it time that settled their dispute? Was she someone he looked up to?*

Bea was a professor, not a doctor, even though she would love to think she had a PhD at the end of her name. Jesse always said she had it out for him. *Is that why she was on the list?* He didn't mean she had it out for him like every other college student. He meant she could care less if he didn't understand the material or why he had to do something for an assignment. She was so wrapped up in proving that her class was the hardest class on campus that she would take points off his project to prove no one was perfect. It was like she was saying that perfection, or anything close to perfection, was a myth and no student could ever achieve a deserving grade. But Jesse was perfect with his work. His passion and pride were undeniably perfect. He listened to her every word and did every part of every assignment. In his world, there was something always to be gained, even when perfection had proven itself. His parents always told him that good enough was never good enough. *Why was she on the list?*

She was a teacher who brought anguish to people's lives. She had her own grading scale, differing from the university's policy so she could easily fail students. She was so stuck on her policies that she forgot the number one objective of being a teacher, student learning. Jesse had a homework assignment that he and his roommate completed together. Three months after they turned it in, she sent them both a message stating that they needed to chat with her about some academic integrity policy violations.

Chapter 20

SHE ENDED UP saying that their homework was similar. *How could something like similar homework be taken so seriously?* I know Jesse well enough to know that he never needed to use someone else to succeed in his schoolwork.

Homework. Not a test. Not a quiz. Homework. We're talking about homework. Not the exam. Not a project. Homework. Homework! Something like homework is similar if the answers are correct. Homework. Something teachers used to check for understanding.

He and his roommate at the time went into her office the next day, and she said that they had copied each other's paper and they would both be receiving a letter home stating that they cheated. I know this must have killed him. Especially since his parents were so uptight about things like that. *I bet they would have punished him as if he was still staying at home, but he lived on his own now.* The crazy part is that he was the type of person to follow through with his parent's discipline even when they weren't around to enforce the rules. They could have told him anything, and he would do as they said, exactly as they said it.

My thoughts about this professor were disgraceful. She caused an overwhelming pain in Jesse's life, and she was searching for people to worship her as a higher human being. I hated arrogance like that. I hated arrogance in the ignorant people who truly believe they have attained a higher status. It seemed her arrogance was the foundation of her stubbornness. When people are this supercilious, they waste their whole life trying to prove something about themselves that they are not. The energy wasted on this unattainable satisfaction increases the height of their wall of stubbornness. This may be the reason she is constantly angry. She wasted all of her time trying to prove a false identity. Like a boxer after he missed a punch. Throwing a punch and missing takes three times the amount of energy it takes to throw a punch and land it on the face of the opponent. She was swinging and missing with one hand but ready to throw another punch with the other hand. She had to be worn out by now.

He told me that when it was over, he ended up taking the blame for the whole thing, he suffered by taking ten percent off his final grade, and he had to write a five-page paper on academic integrity policies. I found his paper on his computer in our room.

Jesse had to write about academic integrity policy violations. He had to have at least two credible sources. It was an assignment that proved Bea's struggle to gain respect from her colleagues and her students.

Journal Entry

Jesse Saunders C grade student Sarcasm and lies are all the same

I am a Cheater

Dishonesty and unfaithful students are multiplying by the second. Dishonesty usually starts at an early age over things that have little meaning. We as teachers have to make sure there is not a trend going on with this negative characteristic of life. I have always been a liar and a cheater. I am a scumbag when it comes to honesty and trust. I feel like I am not ready for the real world after I graduate because of my dishonesty. I also believe that there is no correcting my ways. I will always be this way, and there is no way out. Unfortunately, the facts in this article about statistical cheating and dishonesty paint a vivid image of me and my lifestyle.

Clip off my angel wings because I am liar, a fake, and a cheat. This article explains how unethical, dishonest, and irresponsible behavior destroy a person. Although I have never cheated on an exam, this paper shows that exam cheating is of way more importance than any homework assignment.

I remember the first time I had your class I was convicted of not doing my references in the right format, which ended up initially giving me a D in the course. I had to plead to rewrite the references on my final project to finally get the A that I deserved. I cheated on a homework assignment, and once again you caught me. These are my only times I have ever cheated in college, and I have the reputation of being a two-faced liar.

This article tells us about how to identify a possible cheater in a multiple-choice exam setting and procedures on how to handle someone like me who cheats on assignments. There are so many different aspects and styles of cheating, which may include plagiarism, stealing a test, fabricating academic documents, purchasing term papers, or copying from someone else's exam (Pincus and Schmelkin 2003). This article evaluated how faculty and students conceptualize academic dishonesty and noted two dimensions.

I want you to read this article because I feel like you have forgotten this concept of teaching. The next article relates to a continuum of "seriousness" (i.e., the degree of severity), and the other includes exam- versus paper-related dishonest behavior (Pincus and Schmelkin 2003). I think that you would really like the part about the seriousness of cheating. It talks about how the degree of severity should be taken into consideration when something puts up a red flag and how overreaction from either party could hurt the life of the student forever. I feel that this article is very important. It is important because the honesty levels are damaged, and damaged goods, such as honesty, can never be healed. I hope the only teacher who has ever accused me of cheating still finds me at least twenty percent honest (because that's how much I am being honest with you).

Although this article is mostly about exam cheating, more or less multiple-choice exam cheating, it says nothing about homework and cheating on papers that are done at home. It is very interesting because I can relate very well. I also found that cheating can hurt student learning but <u>a strong campaign</u> can hurt the teaching worse.

I'm basically saying that teachers who become overly concerned about making sure everyone's assignments, even homework, are their own can actually have an extremely negative effect on student learning and a teacher's teaching. There has to be an optimal level of controlling, managing, teaching, and creating. As a future teacher I am going to make sure that I am not solely looking for cheaters and copiers but actually work on showing the students a good example and leading by this example.

I will also make sure that I give all my students equal amounts of attention. This paper also tries to explain why cheating is bad. Cheating is bad because the smarter students and more successful students feel that there is an unequal advantage to the slacker students who copied their papers. When this problem occurs, cheating needs to be an importance to the teacher who makes sure that there is a correction in behavior. In making sure that there is a correction in behavior, great teachers talk one on one with the student in a calm, assertive way. The most terrible teachers will threaten the students with the horrible things in cheating, saying it will damage them for the rest of their life.

Teachers who try to scare students make me sick! I think it is teachers who scare students into corrective ways that cause students not to care about their lives anymore, and cheating becomes the first step into them leading a terrible life. After reading this article, I have come to realize that it is all about the teacher. A teacher who tries to control every little mess up has a negative effect on the student's life. Also, the teacher that tries to scare the shit out of students to correct their behavior has a negative effect on cheating and dishonesty in their students.

As stated in the paper, students agree that cheating is unethical, but the mass majority of college students cheat. In four years of college I have seen plenty of cheating, in exams, homework (if the teacher considers it cheating), quizzes, and especially online postings or quizzes. For some students it is the only way to get a passing grade, the only way to complete the assignment within the amount of time allotted, or many other circumstances. Only a small percentage of cheaters are identified and sanctioned. Generally, educational institutions avoid the procedures for handling cheating, perhaps because they are unworkable in practice. Hard evidence is often lacking, and students may appeal. Mistaken accusations may lead to lawsuits (Dwyer and Hecht 1996). This statement is where the teacher, who takes everything way too seriously when it comes to cheating, can see why and how their actions affect students.

If only a small percentage are caught and you are the stickler teacher who tries to catch everyone cheating, then you are not only doing an awful job at catching the students who are cheating, but you are also forgetting the most important aspect of teaching—student learning. This kind of teacher will find it hard for their students to grasp the objectives of their lesson. You can't catch everyone, but you can be the teacher who leads by example with the behavior modification/management skills that you are teaching to students. Hypocrisy in teaching makes the new information taught to students go in one ear and out of the other.

The interview process for academic integrity violations should be professional, quick, and easy. The teacher brings in the evidence, and the students suspected of cheating come in for a meeting, privately; that is when they engage into the political side of teaching. The assumption by the teacher must start as neutral, and they should just identify the problems they have with the exam and how having the same wrong answers could have happened if someone else was copying them without their knowledge. More than likely the student copied the other student. Then the teacher should tell them politely that the seriousness of their acts can be very detrimental to their grade. The teacher that wants to bring in more power for their own self-worth will threaten the students without full knowledge of the extremities of the sanction. For example, a teacher tells you that you could fail their course and be put back for a whole year because of an assignment, when she has no clue about academic integrity policy.

Teachers who want to scare students to make themselves seem more powerful should change their careers or go back to school to change their major. With such a distasteful reputation they do not deserve to be associated with the school. The interview continues with the teacher not making the student feel like a criminal, even though I have experienced otherwise. In one case, the student does not admit cheating. In that circumstance, the process stops and the student receives the original exam score. Reasoning for this is that, although the statistics indicate that cheating is likely, such probability testing will not hold up alone in a quasi-legal proceeding (Dwyer and Hecht 1996). This statement proves that the teacher who does not feel like it's important to give out sanctions and are more concerned with making sure student learning has occurred are the ones that will be great teachers.

Here is another statement in this paper to prove that once more, Bea, you are an example of what they are talking about. "We wanted to handle identified cheating as a learning experience instead of an administrative procedure. The positive relationship between a teacher and student is too easily damaged when the teacher steps into the role of policing" (Moore 1991).

Once again, thanks for this assignment. It proved to me how much I think of you as a terrific teacher and how awful of a student I am as a liar. I have learned a lot from you about what to do and especially what not to do, whether you intended it or not. I hope you appreciate the care I took in reading these articles and presenting my ideas. Thanks for the hard work, Bea! Now I know that I'm a compulsive liar.

Chapter 21

HE FOUND ARTICLES about teachers who take their policies and rules to the extreme and forget the number one goal of being a teacher is to help students to gain new knowledge and grow. He used references from articles written by scholars who had studied teachers who were too involved with their management and policies. Bea was not expecting a paper like this. She was the only person I knew who could create a situation that would make even the most honest person in the world, a sarcastic liar. In five pages, he showed Bea she was so focused on her reputation that she forgot about student learning.

The overall logline and presentation of this paper would be so attractive to people among the mainstream public. Most people support the confident little guy who seems to have no chance of winning but gives a big '"screw you" anyway. The little guy may not have a fighting chance to win, but his words would at least smack the face of the opponent once or twice. The good guy gives the enemy a taste of assurance because he knows he is right even though he has little chance to succeed. We all like that story. We enjoy his arrogance.

Of course I looked at this paper and thought Jesse won. He

enjoyed writing this paper. When his parents learned of his response, they didn't like it very much. *It's funny how they tried to act like parents who cared when their reputation was at stake.* His parents were especially upset when he got the first B of his life. His parents always pushed him too much. *For God's sakes he got a B. Its not like he failed and became a drug addict.* He always pushed himself too hard to make them proud.

I remembered Jesse telling me what happened the next day. *This one scene is my favorite part. It's the good guy beating the bad guy scene.* He was walking down the hall the day after he turned in the paper when she stopped him by saying, "Jesse, we need to talk about this paper you submitted to me." I started mimicking the role of Bea the professor. I stood up really tall with my back straight and my powerful voice.

This was my favorite part. It brings a smile to my face every time I think about it. I started walking like Jesse did. I walked with a smile and the insecurities of a college freshman doing his first public speech to his classmates. I walked with a presence that brought light to everyone's darkness. I walked like I had someone to help.

He probably wanted to say he was sorry right after he said it, but he did not stop walking. "I don't think we have to talk about anything. I don't have any more classes with you so I don't have to pretend I like you anymore." *Burning bridges smell wonderful when the unexpected words burn the person too.*

The reason I liked it so much was because Jesse wasn't that kind of person who said things like that. *The situation with the professor triggered another personality for Jesse, but only for that instant.* This professor got to Jesse.

Even with the punishment he had suffered he still felt bad about what he said. He was too nice to people like Professor Bea. *Maybe he saw her as the kind of teacher he never wanted to be.* He had a heart that was way too vulnerable. When a heart is on the sleeve, it's easily injured by those who care nothing for it. He could say "I hate you" in his own manipulative way and still apologize for it, even if his target was too dim-witted to figure out what he meant.

Chapter 22

I SCHEDULED A meeting with Bea. The campus was empty, the professors were out on fall break, and the building was vacant, except for this professor's office. *How many ways could she try to make herself seem like royalty?* Scheduling a meeting and making me wait as she sat there in her office doing nothing. Rather than wait submissively like a peasant patiently waiting for her majesty, I wandered off.

I felt myself becoming Jesse as I walked down the hall. *That's probably where he said that response to her. Yeah, I bet he was walking right there and she tried to stop him here. Then I could see him bitch-slap her with words as he walked down these steps.*

Jesse didn't have a lot of friends, but a lot of people knew of him. I worried he wouldn't have a reason to live if he didn't have a lot of people who knew him. As I walked down the hall, I began to act like I was Jesse and imagined the tables and chairs were people. I walked down the stairs saying "Hey" to the people he once knew, but nothing more. I was on a first-name basis with everyone passing. *We pretend to be interested in people's lives, saying, "Hey, how are you doing?" We think that we're being polite. Sometimes being polite protects us from the truth behind people.* He probably knew more about them then he knew about himself. *I wonder if he did not know a lot of people because he never went to very many social gatherings.* I begged and begged for him to come out to social outings with me, though he wasn't that type to open up to people. He was just starting to open up to me before he was murdered.

He had a lot of people he considered friends, but how many were lifetime friends? How many of his friends really knew Jesse? He needed something else from these people. He needed a deeper connection with people.

Nobody really knew Jesse except for the select group of people on the list. The people on the list knew him really well. They knew him better than I did. The people on the list had a chance to stop this from happening. *Why would a teacher that once screwed him over be on the list?* She wouldn't have been on my list. *Maybe I misunderstood the list.* The list could be people he hated. Then again he never hated anyone. Abby was still his lover and whether she was here or there wasn't going to change his feelings for her. I needed to understand the meaning of the list. *Why were these people on it? Why did he make this list in the first place? Why weren't they able to stop this?*

Chapter 23

MY MIND HAD drifted off, but I remembered the real reason I was here so I turned around. Approaching her office, I could sense why he felt animosity for her. She had the stench of hate and negativity. With the anger I felt from being kept waiting, I fully understood their relationship's ups and downs now. She was negative and cynical. He was positive and sanguine. Those two styles don't match. I could tell just by the mere smell of the room that she was stubborn. *It was her way or no way at all.*

Even though their personalities were grossly opposed, he still respected her. She had the job he dreamed of having. He wanted to touch all the people he possibly could in his lifetime. He once told me if he taught at a school where he saw seven hundred students a week, by the end of his thirty-year career he would have directly impacted more than thirty thousand people of tomorrow.

He was not only interested in teaching young students, he also wanted to teach others how to teach so he could play it forward through his education students as they took what they learned throughout the world. He could touch even more lives that way.

I took a deep breath as I looked at the door I was about to walk through. When I entered her dark, oppressive office, I knew we would not be friends at the end of this meeting. She was too arrogant and not yet been put her in her place yet. She had pictures of herself everywhere, from all around the world. She was always by herself. *Was she lonely?* What did it matter? I was getting ready to be brutally honest with this professor, and I wasn't going to feel sorry for her not having any friends.

Had I absorbed the revulsion Jesse once felt for this person? Had this animosity bled into my veins?

Chapter 24

"HELLO SIR," THE sound coming from her lips left me with a repugnant, distasteful appetite. I could understand now how even Jesse could hate this person. There was something in her words that made me feel like I was an ankle-biter while she was one of the crowned heads. The superiority conveyed in those two words drowned out my thoughts, distracting me from my purpose in being there. She was a suspect, and I needed to know why Jesse was killed. I knew she brought him a lot of pain and despair when they had their arguments over homework. I imagined him looking up to her, placing her in high standing, only to be let down. She became the model of exactly what he *never* wanted to become.

All he wanted to be was accepted. Jesse never totally changed himself for anyone. I could tell this woman was the cause for so many sleepless nights in his dorm. Jesse had a superiorly flexible foundation to his personality. Although he adjusted his personality for other people so they would consider him a friend, there were certain morals and rules he lived by and that would never change.

"Are you okay?" As if she really cared. She wouldn't care if I died right here, right now on her office room floor.

"You seemed to black out standing up." She had an English

accent, which might have been the reason that I sensed royalty coming from her. She was probably not as bad as I thought.

"How do you do, Professor?" I attempted to make my southern accent have a quality equal to her standard of speech. I needed her to let me in.

"I am well. Now tell me why we are here today?" She was straight to the point. I could tell she would be the alpha male in her lesbian relationship.

"Tell me about Jesse?" I wanted to hear her perspective of him, although I would probably throw her opinion into the garbage as soon as I left her office. I didn't plan to change my mind about Jesse, but I was aware I only knew the real Jesse through his notebook.

"What a terrible loss this school experienced when he died. Did you know him? He was on track to becoming a great teacher. I remember pushing him relentlessly in the books. He was as hard of a worker as I could ever imagine myself being." Her statement was contradictory, mixing arrogance with sensitivity. Figuring this suspect out was proving to be difficult. I wanted to hate her so badly. But I could not.

"Yes, I knew him." I kept my response short, still confused about her opening statement.

"Okay, so you know how driven he was?"

Why was she being nice? Am I missing something? I was expecting her to say things, like Jesse was very rebellious and we never got along in any of our classes. Jesse was always challenging my judgment and never did exactly as he was told. He would do exactly what he thought was the right to him. Where were the confessions like that?

She was so straight to the point at the beginning of the conversation. I had to reach past this seemingly sensitive part of her. I had to be aware that she may feign a false sense of fondness for him now that he was dead. I know she did.

I decided that I wasn't going to hear what I needed to hear, unless

I put the evidence I knew out there.

"Yes, I know most things about Jesse. I was really close to him outside of school. Tell me what Jesse was like in your classroom." *Was he defiant? Was he always challenging your wits?*

"Well, Jesse and I had a different kind of teacher-student relationship than usual. He was very interested in expanding all of my boundaries ..."

I can feel her covering up the real truth in an effort to protect her status. I let myself think about where Jesse sat in the classroom. *I bet he sat in the front because that would make it easier for him to challenge the teacher's positions. I bet he knew more about the subjects of the classes than the professors did.*

"He and another student in the class had basically copied each other's homework word for word. I had to make an example out of those two boys. I wanted this assignment to not only be a punishment, but something that they could learn from, being as they all wanted to be teachers. Brad turned in a beautifully written paper about how cheating at an early age could cause damage to the adult life of that child unless it was stopped right away by the teacher. On the other hand, there was Jesse's paper."

I knew that the paper would come up in this conversation; I just didn't know when or how she would say it. I was going to like this part. This was the part where her conceit disintegrated as if it was smashed into a rock at full speed.

"Can you believe that he turned in a paper like that to a university council professor? I was appalled at this blatant defiance." She chuckled as if expecting me to join her.

"Are you sure you're okay? Your eyes appeared to be rolling into the back of your head."

I tried to fake a smile so that she would continue.

I kept silent because I could tell she enjoyed hearing herself talk. But she didn't keep talking about Jesse. She just kept going on and on about my health.

"Listen, I am a competent investigator."

I didn't have to prove myself to her! Why should I care what she thought about my job or my ability to solve cases? Is she trying to weaken my pride? Why was I letting her get to me? I could feel myself becoming more defensive than I should. In order to keep me from seeing her insecurity she went on the offensive. She's a manipulator. That's how she got through to Jesse. That's how she killed him.

Chapter 25

"Carry on, please." I calmed down for the sake of this investigation's continuance.

"Well, Jesse had a problem with authority sometimes."

This bitch is lying. If my face were a piece of paper it would read, "Tell me the truth and cut out the fat." *He didn't have a problem with authority, just a problem with people who demanded more than they should. Like you. But I couldn't say that.* I had to get the truth and nothing else.

"Sometimes he came into class very happy and pretended to enjoy class. But most times he didn't like class. He must have thought he didn't need the classes he was taking. If anyone could skip every day of class and pass, it would be him, I admit. He was very intelligent. His intellect could be very intimidating. For the first time in my life I felt academically inferior."

She had swallowed her pride but only for one sentence. She immediately regained her overconfidence.

"My class is one of the few classes on campus that has a high failure rate. I prepare these students to be top-notch teachers, and I have high expectations."

There it is. Come out and play bitch. Give me your honesty. Say what your confused mind wants to say. I was making her uncomfortable and was willing to take only so much of this dick-measuring conversation, especially when she showed me the grading scale that she used in all of her classes.

"I know. I remember him talking about your class and how *hard* it was." This was an insult that she would probably not realize until I left. I was having fun now. I was laughing inside. I have finally found the upper hand I have been looking for in this conversation.

"I have been nominated for many awards."

"I'm sorry, what does this have to do with Jesse?" I gave her a smirk that could have ended the discussion if she had noticed it. I had to keep the questioning on the right track.

"I know my policies and rules are a little strict, but I know how to keep a good, respectful relationship with my students. To be a master teacher you must know how to establish boundaries first and then connect with the students. Classroom management is where I excel at teaching. When I eventually had a conversation with Jesse and he realized that I wasn't as bad a teacher as he presumed, I convinced him to apologize. He even asked me to write a letter of reference for him. He wanted a career like mine. I was like a role model for him. I can't believe he …"

"I know. His murder surprised us all."

I had to interrupt because I always felt the need to finish someone's sentence when I knew exactly what they were going to say. I gave them a kind of newspeak when their answer on the headlines was wrong. I needed something more.

Chapter 26

"What was it about Jesse that made him the way he was?" *Yes, tell me, lady. Why was he smarter than you? Why were you on the list?*

"Jesse was a very special individual who just wanted to help others. He called me one night very late."

The first part of the conversation kept this investigation moving in the right direction. This next part was the whole reason I came here to talk to her.

"He seemed troubled. Like something was bothering him. He told me I was someone he looked up to. I wasn't used to hearing that. I almost felt bad about what I did."

"Wait, you talked to him?"

Finally she gave me something that was worth hearing. She took her time getting to this part of our conversation. If she talked to him, then I knew she was the killer.

"No, he left a message."

"Please tell me what he said."

He said, "I wanted you to know through all of these tough times in our relationship I still looked up to you. As much as I challenged your teaching and never gave you the credit that you deserved, I looked up to you. It's just like you said. I'll never be a teacher with

95

my acts of defiance. I'll never be a teacher now. Good-bye."

She had a foot in this race now. As far as I had known, Jesse only left five words on everyone else's voicemail. He was trying to say something to her. He tried to get some point across. *I needed to find why she was on the list and why he left her that message.*

"Even on a message he would still find a way to show his insubordination. His compliment was meant to be sarcastic."

This was why I had to finish these interrogations. I had to find out everything about each one on the list.

Silently forgiving her arrogance once again in spite of finding more about the truth, I asked, "What did he mean by saying he'll never be a teacher? Did you have something to do with that?"

Depending on her answer, I was thinking about all of the evidence I had against her. She could've manipulated this whole scheme, so I had to be careful.

She spoke less arrogantly now. *The devil may actually feel something after all.*

"I gave him the reference he requested. I thought that he would take them and tear them up in my face or something. I didn't know how serious he was about these reference letters."

She looked down as if she were ashamed. I started to feel the smoky wind from flames inside of me escape.

If she were looking into my eyes right now she would see how green eyes turn to red. My glare was the laser of a gun, pointing in the direction of her heart of stone.

I spoke slowly and with strong conviction, "What did the letters say?"

I couldn't tell exactly what her eyes were doing, but I knew that they were holding back tears. "They said Jesse was very enthusiastic about teaching. He was the best and brightest student here at the university. I wouldn't doubt that he had all of the content knowledge that one could in an undergraduate program. He was top of his class in every subject matter. He was a leader who always got the job done. But he still needed more time to grow. He had a very defiant attitude in the classroom, and he lacked ability to listen to authority."

I clutched the notebook I used for jotting down notes. The binding began to make cracking noises. I had Jesse's death grip from yesterday.

"How could you? He didn't get a call back from any of the interviews because of you!"

I allowed my voice to rise up to make my point clear. This was the real reason she killed him.

"It was a difficult situation. I had to give prospective employers the truth."

This set me off the edge.

"Your truth was about keeping your pride. Keeping your dignity! Not about what it should have been about. What about his volunteer hours? What about his love for teaching? Love for people? Love for living? You stole something that can never be given back. I hope you know what you've done. You have torn him apart more than you will ever know. I am convinced that his death had something to do with what you've done."

I had to get through the entire list before making accusations, but I knew she was guilty.

"I did what I had to do. It wasn't an easy situation."

"Yes it was. You could have been like every one of his other professors who gave him a letter of reference, glorifying his achievements and his enthusiasm. Why do you constantly feel the need to prove your superiority to people?"

"I don't expect you to understand making diplomatic decisions. This is a business and nothing is pretty in politics."

"Save the bullshit, lady. I have enough of it burying me from the half-truth you've been giving me all morning."

"You should leave."

I will gladly. I got what I needed from her.

"Thank you, Professor Bea. You have been a great suspect."

I knew the allegation would get her attention.

I listened hard for her next words, because for once throughout this whole conversation, she finally heard me. Typical of most people today, she did not listen when someone else spoke. She was too busy thinking about what she was going to say next. We are so involved in ourselves we do not listen and learn something from someone else. How can we think we are living when we are too self-centered to listen to another person's words? All was quiet for about fifteen seconds.

"It has been an experience, Mr ..." She wore her conceited smirk with a slight sign of defeat.

"Call me Jesse."

Did she finally choke on one of her words? She was ready to say her next witty response, but those words were sucked back down and now they were stuck in her throat. I hoped the words were so sharp that they cut through her throat so she would suffer the most painful death possible. I hoped terrible things would happen to her.

I couldn't end the investigation now. I needed to interrogate four more people before I pulled the plug. In addition, this would then be considered a short story and not be given the respect of a novel. I couldn't do that.

No response.

I won.

Chapter 27

HE DRIVES LIKE he's done this before. *Maybe he is really afraid on the inside and doesn't want to show anyone that he isn't comfortable. I know that if I was in this situation I would be scared out of my mind. Not only about the health reasons and how close we were to losing our lives right here in this very car; but even if we didn't crash, we could be taken by them.* I had better make conversation with him.

"I like this album, but what's with all the interludes? If I buy a CD, I want to hear music, not someone talking." Making conversation was hard with him. Music was something that he was very passionate about. He could talk for days about his musical tastes.

"Come on man. 'In Frail Wings of Vanity and Wax' was good, but 'The Emptiness' just proves their artistic capabilities. I mean, how many bands make something meaningful on the radio these days? None!"

I knew that would get him going.

Part III

SAVING MORE. LIVING LESS.

Journal Entry

"They told me she was going to be okay. I was so thankful that my best friend was okay too. I don't know what I would have done if either of them got hurt. Two words filled me up to describe every inch of my human life right now, guilt and disgrace. It doesn't help when my parents decided not to come to the hospital for me. Luckily, she came to pick me up. Why does she understand our friendship and my parents don't? What was I doing wrong?

I looked out of my broken windshield, praying that this whole thing was a dream. The airbags deployed. I remember seeing them deflated and hanging out. Until this night I have always thought all airbags were white; like in movies. I started to hit my face repeatedly, hoping I wouldn't feel one of the blows to my head. I wanted the gray airbags to be a sign that this was a nightmare. I wanted my best friend to stop bleeding. I wanted the car I hit to un-dent itself. I wanted my car to go in reverse. I wanted to not be so mad when I put the keys in my car. I'm sorry.

I needed this situation to have a restart button like in my video games. Sometimes I wished my life had the ability to restart. I could try new things with no risk. I could see my life in third person. I could see who my friends were. I could die and see who truly cared.

I bought flowers to bring to her. She only had small bruises and a broken arm, and she was going to be okay. I knew she would probably be mad at me, but I had to show her that I was sorry. I wanted her to feel my remorse. I hoped she would accept my apology. I shouldn't have been driving like that.

I called my best friend tonight, and he seemed to be okay. He told me his mother was worse than he was. She got a phone call from the policeman about thirty minutes after it all happened. She fainted and hit her head on a counter, but she was going to be fine. I felt responsible for her injuries too. I'm glad everyone was alive. I don't know what I would have done if anyone was seriously hurt. I would probably never drive again and feel forever in debt to all of the people I hurt.

God, thank you for not taking anyone up with you tonight because I couldn't handle being responsible for the end of someone's life. I hope you look after them with all of your power. You helped me tonight. I understand the lesson you taught me. I should never drive as upset as I was tonight. You helped me in the hospital because all of my aches and pains were held at bay until I knew everyone was still alive and moving. I could feel the truth of what really happened as soon as the doctor told me they were all right. I felt the pain of ignorance. I know I needed that pain from you because everyone needs the pain of punishment to remember what they learned. I will always remember this pain as a gift from you because the weightiness of my choices should not go unnoticed. I love you and thank you for waiting to take them up there with you."

Chapter 28

WALKING OUT OF her office built my confidence in the case. As of right then, she was at the top of my list. She was my number one suspect, the only one with a true motive to kill Jesse. I guess it was easier to hate someone who was near perfect because they are what you want to be. It's almost effortless to envy someone. She hated that he was an A+ student. She looked for anything to pin something negative on his positive attitude. *Why could she not be like every other teacher? Why could she not embrace his person?* The bottom line was that she caused Jesse a lot of heartache. He questioned whether he really wanted to be a teacher any more after his first class with her. Still, he was a better person than I could ever be; I would have never called her.

My car was parked in the parking lot for the recreation center, which was closed for the holiday. I thought I would have been the only person driving on campus, but obviously I was not. A yellow ticket on my windshield showed me that I was not alone.

"Son of a bitch!" I moved into a slight jog to my car.

You have got to be kidding me. I hated a lot of things about the university already, but this added to the pile. I didn't let the ridiculous parking ticket bother me too long because Jesse wouldn't.

Every aspect of my life had to mimic his if I wanted to get the truth.

Chapter 29

I DROVE BACK to my apartment to collect my mind. I had more questions for the next suspects. I was the type of person who needed to write everything down or else I would forget it all, or at least some significant detail.

When I got back to the apartment, I wrote down notes from the previous suspects' interrogations. I wrote down only the essentials about my time with them. I wrote little down that they said. Most of my notes were based on what I thought about their personalities and their behavior when they talked about Jesse. Abby looked down as if she regretted leaving him. I could tell she truly missed him. She showed it all over her face. I hated when people tried to protect the memory of the dead, but when Abby did it, she meant it. I put her on the bottom on the list and my preconceptions of her disappeared. Bea chuckled and started to grin when she talked about Jesse, and I hated that. She chuckled only in a way that a true butch lesbian would chuckle before speaking. She hated her students, especially Jesse. Her English accent bothered me as well. It made her sound as arrogant as the body language she portrayed.

I stopped writing about the past interviews and found the paper I wrote on that terrible night that I woke up. On a short list of names I found another name of the responsible, Georgio the pool man. Georgio was the owner of the neighborhood pool. He had a knack for numbers. He knew how to save his money and how to spend it. He knew when to buy secure investments. Jesse was his go-to guy for anything at the pool. He did everything Georgio asked and more. Jesse was only given a twenty hour a week schedule because that was the only position Georgio could give him. Jesse received pay for twenty hours a week, but he worked over forty.

Jesse volunteered countless hours for the neighborhood's swim team at the pool. All of the parents loved having him as a volunteer coach. He honed his teaching skills at the pool. It was like being a kid at a playground for him.

In these hard economic times, Georgio had done pretty well for himself. He was a penny pincher. Jesse admired him dearly. He would tell me about the things Georgio taught him. Jesse was trying to teach me how to become some kind of sustainable wealth accumulator. I didn't have the patience to listen to him. But Jesse listened to everything Georgio said to him. Georgio made a big impression on him.

He told Jesse, "At your age, you should be saving a quarter for every dollar you spend. That quarter you save now will turn into financial freedom when you're fifty-nine and half."

Needless to say, Jesse had a retirement plan at the age of seventeen. *Who has a retirement plan at seventeen years old?* Georgio molded Jesse into a younger version of himself. He wanted to provide a bright financial future for Jesse. *Jesse had a retirement account with eight thousand, two hundred thirty-nine dollars and twenty-two cents when he died; he had a bright financial future.*

Chapter 30

WORKING AT THE pool was not the same as teaching. He wanted to teach more than the basics of swimming. He wanted to teach the children everything. Not just the major subjects like math, reading, writing, history, and science; he wanted to teach them life skills. He was going to be that teacher who showed the students how to have good character. He could teach them how to live a fulfilling life.

Even in this economy, he couldn't be a volunteer teacher because it was too much of a liability issue for a school to have him on campus. Any kind of work facility worried about the risk of a volunteer getting injured because they wouldn't be able to pay the insurance companies. *He couldn't give away his free services.*

This world we lived in had become dangerously bureaucratic. Everything was backed up by a policy. These policies and liabilities had too many logistics and not enough logic. It reminded me of what Jesse said to Bea, only it applies to the world, "When the world is too hung up on policies and management we will forget the number one objective of being on this world, living."

Jesse had a great deal of trouble finding a job as a teacher. Every interview was followed by short letters with tall disappointments. He was highly qualified, but he still had difficulty finding a job.

There had to be something he was missing. Something he wasn't doing in the interview. Or maybe it was something to do with his schoolwork. But he was top of his class and he volunteered the most hours, compared to any of his fellow students. He definitely had the qualifications he needed, so what else could it be? I thought that perhaps it had to do with the interviewer's first impression. *I imagine the principal saw a shy, insecure man when Jesse walked through the door. He was probably smiling, but that would not be enough. He had so much trouble getting past his social anxiety. If only they knew what kind of person he was with children.*

Because of national budget cuts in education, Jesse couldn't find a job opening for new teachers. You needed to have experience to get hired. *How was he supposed to have professional teaching experience when he had just graduated college?* The professors were excellent in teaching education theory but they did not teach job interview skills. They were cutting and transferring teachers to and from schools, causing classes to be overfilled. *But for what?* It's not fair for the students, or the teachers, to be in a classroom with fifty other children. This overcrowded environment was completely wrong, but even with fifty students, Jesse would have found a way to reach out to each one of them.

It was a surprisingly hard market. A market that we all used to think was secure. We believed it was something that could never fail. Teaching was something that we valued in this world, something that we thought had great job security, now and forever. We used to care about our future, but now it seemed the objective is how much money we could save. *When experienced teachers were getting laid off everywhere, how was a graduate supposed to get a job? I wondered, if Georgio was in charge of all this, would he make these same budget cuts as well?*

Chapter 31

WHEN I WALKED into the lobby at the pool, I knew that this was going to be a different scene than the last. This one was going to be heartfelt. I could tell because of the love in the room. *I've never walked into a room and just felt like all of the love I ever had in my life was mixed in with the paint. There was love in the colors of the walls. There was love in the cleanliness of the floors. Georgio took ownership of, shared that love with others who walked into the room.* I took ownership of this love. This room was peaceful. I haven't had that since that terrible night.

Georgio was sitting at his desk, probably working out his budget for the week. He looked like he was in his mid to upper forties, addicted to working even when he wasn't there. I imagined he was probably single and deeply wanted a son to carry on his name.

I remembered that Jesse and Georgio talked about opening up a new business in backyard pools and pool maintenance. That wasn't Jesse's first choice of a career, but Georgio was a father figure and an intelligent financial planner. He trusted Georgio with his life. *Maybe that was Georgio's plan all along.*

I'm sure he was just giving Jesse a safety net in case he didn't find a teaching job. I didn't know much about their pool business plans, but something about it bothered me enough to come here. *So did the phone call. Maybe he thwarted Jesse's attempts of finding a job because he wanted him to himself.*

"Hello sir. Please have a sit." He spoke with a dubious confidence. The force behind those words seemed hollow.

The paper he was looking at made it seem like he wrote a script out before I came. I knew he had been expecting me, although he didn't even look up to see who had walked through his door. He was too cheap to buy a surveillance camera system. There was no way he saw me coming in. I guess I was on time. He probably planned to budget his time for which way the wind blew next.

"Tell me about the time you spent with Jesse." It was hard to say Jesse with such a past tense. *I didn't want him to go. I wanted to speak of him in the now, the present.*

"Well … Jesse was a great kid. I loved him like a son. In fact, I was more of a father to him than his own father."

I thought I knew Jesse's life, but before I read his journals, I would have never guessed he'd say anything bad about his parents. *So how did this man know about them?*

I had to interrupt.

"How do you know his parents? What were they like?"

I wasn't speaking as if they were already dead but as though they were no longer his parents anymore. *I wondered if he thought they, or someone they paid, killed Jesse. He might be willing to help me find them.*

"They were extremely strict parents who enjoyed him having very few friends. It was a harsh way to raise a kid. They always assumed public school was the death of all children's dreams. Even though they were financially well off, they still couldn't afford private school. They could have prioritized differently to pay for private school, but they had their big house, which they thought was an asset. The house was obviously way too expensive for them. If they had only invested ten percent of their money for Jesse's education, he would have been able to go to private school, and college, without Jesse having to pay a dime."

"What about his friends in high school? What were they like? Were any of them a bad influence?"

I needed an adult's perspective to see where the lies and truths fit. Jesse's life could be interpreted many different ways. *I was still the only one claiming his death as a murder.*

"He had very few friends, but the friends he had were genuinely good kids. Kids who would not consider partying too hard, drinking a suicide-style soda and French fries all night until three A.M." I was very in tune to the word *suicide. That* word has followed me around like the wild neighborhood cat that I kept feeding.

I was ambivalent about meaning of suicide. To me suicide was the easiest way to reach forever, o*r maybe the hardest.* I think everyone wants to commit suicide to a certain degree. I mean, there is a spectrum of suicidal intentions. On one hand, you have someone who merely wants the hours in the day to go by faster; that's when killing time becomes killing yourself. On the opposite end of the spectrum, you have an intoxicated, lonely person staring at an empty bottle of painkillers, knowing that the combination would be deadly and the pain would end.

I wondered if Jesse thought of suicide before he was killed. I have. It has only been a recent addition to my fatalist ways. His death had more meaning than the casket we buried in the ground. His death was my awakening to helplessness and guilt. I knew that I was not alone with this guilt, and that was the reason I was standing there in that room. *If I'm going down, I'm taking you with me.* Under oath, I will speak the letters that make the specific set of words that build the phrases, which compiled, mean justice.

"They always gave him the hardest problems without a direct path to the right answers. I know it was a hard concept, but if anyone could understand the world best, it was Jesse. He understood it through the light of day rather than the darkness of night. He came over to my house every day to study. I wanted to help him because I genuinely loved him. I only wanted the best for that him ..."

What was the best for Jesse? What did Jesse want? It seemed like everything Jesse did was what other people wanted from him. I don't think he made any choices on his own. *Well, I couldn't say that, because he did choose to stay in the car.*

"… and he didn't come home on time. And you know what they did?"

Good. He never noticed. *I wondered if he ever even looked up.*

I could tell he was unsure. He didn't check to see if I was listening. His face would have told me more than his words, but he didn't look up. His insecurity almost made it seem like he felt what he was saying was not good enough for me to hear. *How could someone who is so good with numbers, who also is very upfront to people about money, lack confidence?*

"No, tell me, sir."

"They grounded him for a month. Can you believe that? He was truly studying economics with me one night and came home four minutes and thirty-seven seconds late. His parents brought new meaning to the word strict."

Thirty-seven seconds. How in the hell did he know that? Everything was numbers with Georgio the pool man.

Chapter 32

"THANK YOU SIR. If I really knew Jesse, what would I know?"

His perspective wasn't just something I needed to hear for the investigation. It was something I wanted to hear. He brought joy back in my life. He allowed me to remember Jesse as he truly was.

"He was the only person who actually listened to my speech about money. I never expected someone to pick up on my financial advice. He was easily convinced about retirement and starting a savings program. I have never been able to reach out to someone like him. He was such a good listener."

"Do you think his friends took advantage of this attribute of his?" It's dangerous to be that trusting.

"I don't think so, because he rationed his friends in high school. He really didn't have any friends that were a bad influence on him."

I wondered if Jesse thought of me as a friend. I hope he did. I hope I wasn't a bad influence on him. Besides money, what kind of influence did Georgio have on him?

"So his friends were limited, but what kind of influence did you have on Jesse?"

I was hoping he would say something about the pool business. If

115

Georgio had influenced him at all to forget his dreams of teaching and become a pool man like himself, then he would move up on the list of suspects. He would have a knife in this fight.

"It's sad to say that I really had nothing else to offer Jesse besides good financial planning advice. I could teach him all of the things he needed to know about the market. I could offer him nothing about teaching children. That's all my father taught me how to do, invest my money."

He passed his test for now, but I would approach this question another way. It was hard to get a decent read on him. His face was like a sample or an advertisement of a product that you dearly wanted to have. I could not tell how good this product was because the sample was too small to make a judgment. His information was not specific. He knew the right answers to my questions, but he had a door shut to the room I wanted to enter. I needed more from him.

"You said his friends were good kids. Do you know any of his friends?" I needed a name. I needed information he had not given me yet.

"He did have a friend that he no longer spoke to after the car wreck. His name was Dontae. As kids, Dontae and Jesse were always on the same basketball team. They hung out together all of the time. Dontae tried to get a job up here, but with our budget cuts and his lack of transportation, it was not possible to keep him on the payroll. He was only available when Jesse was able to drive him. I know that they played a lot of basketball together. He always asked me for information about special grants and scholarships. Every day, Jesse insisted that Dontae was going to get a scholarship to play college ball with him. Jesse liked to dream about how his life would be to play ball in college with his best friend."

He started stuttering, not because he was lying, but because he was crying. When he mentioned grants and scholarships, I guess he thought about how important that must have made him feel. *He was a father figure for Jesse.*

"So what happened to Dontae? Did he move away?"

"One night Jesse was driving and got into a terrible accident. It was amazing that he didn't get seriously hurt. I know that wreck did some bad things to him. He came into work quiet the next day. That day seemed like he didn't feel anything. He was always so full of life and grateful for being alive. He didn't mention anything else about Dontae after that happened. It made me sick to see him like that."

Every single one of these interrogations brought new items to the list of my work. That was why I had to continue. I couldn't wait to share my news with those skeptics when I finish this case.

Chapter 33

I HAD A new suspect. Dontae wasn't on the list. Jesse died at the age of twenty-two. He and Dontae separated as friends at an earlier age. I had to find out more. I had to find more information on that relationship.

"That day was awful. The police were here to talk with him about the wreck. He dropped to his knees when he heard the news they brought. I still don't know what happened. He never clocked out that day, he just left. I made sure I clocked him out though. I gave him a couple of extra minutes, but any more would have been excessive."

"Thank you for that information. Now, can you tell me about this business you guys talked about starting?"

I trusted Georgio. I knew he would answer.

"I told him that if he had any interest, we could start a pool business together."

It was almost like the words "business" and "together" were a dagger in his chest.

"I knew he was having trouble finding a job, and I was only suggesting a backup plan. He could have either taken the job as a career or as a temporary job for him to have."

His voice was cracking.

"He had so much ambition. He had the drive to be an excellent contributor to society. I knew with all of the budget cuts he might not find a teaching job instantly. I never would've thought he would be a victim of such an awful crime."

I don't think Georgio had kids because it was not economically feasible to have kids in his eyes. He probably calculated the cost of raising a kid from the moment of conception through college graduation. Jesse might have been a constant reminder of his decision to remain childless. *Maybe that was a motive to kill him?*

"So you never pressured Jesse into doing this business with you?"

He paused and briefly looked up at me. His eyes were bloodshot and tears darkened his shirt.

"What are you trying to say? I know what you think you're doing, but you have the wrong person here. All I had was Jesse. He was the one thing in my life that made me realize every day I breathed could be better. He was my hope ... I never gave him an ultimatum. I told him that we would wait until mid-October. If he didn't have a teaching job by then, he could look into doing this business with me."

I trusted his answer and felt bad for assuming the worst. "Please carry on about Jesse."

"Did you know that he paid half of his college tuition while he was in school?"

This was his way of forgiving me. He changed the negative to a positive memory.

"I can't tell you how much money he saved from student loan interest. I mean, student loan interest can add up to ten percent of the loan, and then people wait to pay it off in four years or longer."

It's funny how he was so wrapped up into the numbers of everything; he constantly forgot about the letters. There's more understanding in letters. Letters make us have meaning. Numbers only add up to letters anyway.

Could Georgio be a suspect anymore? I could tell he felt parental love for Jesse. A sane parent would never kill his own kid. Good parents would do anything for their kid to make them happy and help them to succeed in the world. But then again, his parents were part of the responsible group, so Georgio will remain a suspect until he is proven innocent.

I could see his words were like hands pushing the dagger deeper into his chest cavity, slowly and painfully. He started to collapse.

"Why didn't I pick up the phone? This could've ended and he could still be here. Why? Why? Why? I never got to say good-bye."

As he cried, I knew I wasn't feeling anything close to what he was at that particular moment. I could tell this was a new feeling of desolation for Georgio. It was like he lost a son.

I felt nothing because I guarded myself from it. Emotions can force you to make irrational decisions. I couldn't afford it. I only had my mother. My mother supported anything I did that hinted of enthusiasm. Besides her, no one knows the struggles I was going through emotionally because I wouldn't let them. My job was just to get the suspects to let me in and nothing else. I had no emotion, no feeling.

I wonder if Georgio would want to kill the murderers now that he had reached this rock-bottom grief. *This could be a breakthrough to my theory about grief turning to anger and aggression quicker than any other emotion. But maybe this disproved my theory. Maybe he had reached past the initial sadness into the deepest of sadness, and there wasn't a ladder to climb out of the hole. Or maybe his deepest sadness would eventually turn into the craziest of madness. Maybe he would kill with me.*

Chapter 34

"I'M SORRY ... I just want to be alone."

I finally saw his face. He looked up into my eyes. I felt myself becoming more like Jesse as he commended me on pursuing this investigation.

"I apologize for saying I knew what you were doing as if it were a bad thing. I just get upset when other people assume they know what I've gone through. You're a good man."

"Thank you. You're the first person to say that about my investigation."

Maybe it was his nose that he was so afraid to show. I hated my teeth. He had a crooked nose that looked like it had been broken numerous times. He had this lack of confidence that I only briefly related to lying, but he had been so afraid to look up. *Or maybe he just wasn't confident in his words.*

I had to feel nothing from these interrogations because people could trick you into giving them your empathy. They would do whatever they had to, to make it seem you shared a common ground with them, manipulating you into dropping all suspicions. Some investigators may think that if the suspects carried this much grief, there was no way they were responsible. That wasn't going to happen to me.

"Becky, cancel all my meetings today and tell Pool Side Assistance we're not buying that stock."

I could tell his outer walls were very proficient at securing the internal emotions, that is, until my conversation with him.

He gave me the signal that we were done by putting his hands on the chair and lifting himself up. I got out of my chair and took another look at the paint on the walls. The love I would always remember. There was more lost here than just a pool employee and swim team volunteer. There was a void that couldn't be filled. No one could fill the hole Jesse left as he took his last breath. He was ground zero, except there was no chance a mosque would be built on his broken foundation. Nothing could fill the depression he made.

I started walking with Georgio when an awkward silence was broken by his sulk. I didn't know what else to say to him, besides how much I appreciated the information he had given me.

"Georgio, you have been of great assistance, and I finally have belief in someone. Good-bye."

Georgio wasn't a suspect for now. But I would not let him slide from future accusations later on in my investigation.

I wondered if he was calculating in his meeting with me, even when he had reached this rock-bottom sorrow. *Even in his sorrow, would he still run his life with numbers?* It seemed to me that anger wouldn't be Georgio's motive. If Georgio did kill Jesse, it was because Jesse found a job as a teacher and wouldn't be able to do the pool business with him. I felt almost certain he was not a suspect anymore, but I could not totally rule him out. The constitutional judicial system was different from mine. I governed my life, and this case, as though everyone was guilty until proven innocent. There are too many loopholes in letting them remain innocent while waiting to convict them. It's not until we are bleeding that we feel and give the truth of guilt. I was here to make them all bleed.

Chapter 35

I HAD A good interview with Georgio. He gave me a name that might help me solve this case. I just needed to find how to get in contact with him.

Finding him took days. I checked Jesse's cell phone and he had no number saved for him. I called people from his high school, and they didn't know where Dontae was. I theorized about why his contact information took so long to find. I couldn't stop thinking about the worse possible scenarios. *I wondered what the police said to Jesse that made him drop to his knees. Did he do time in prison for the wreck? Did he die in that car?* It had to be something about someone else. Something was missing, and Dontae might have that missing puzzle piece.

I sat in the dorm with all of Jesse's contact information on his friends. I had a desk full of journals, phone numbers, addresses, and pictures. I had a certain ritual. Anytime I saw him in a picture I marked his face out with a black Sharpie marker. It didn't help; I still see his face everywhere. I saw his face when I closed my eyes. I saw his face in the words coming out of the mouths of the suspects on the list, especially mine.

Finally, I had something to write home about. I found a dusty yearbook of Jesse's. I ordinarily would not have thought to look through it, but thought he may have comments from his friends on the blank pages in the back. I became excited in the darkest way possible. I found an address. Dontae had written in the back of his yearbook with his name, number, and address.

Ride or Die Bros 4 life. 3898 Brian Jordan Pl.

I saw the address but couldn't find a picture or a last name for Dontae. *Was he not in high school yet? Had he graduated already?* I even looked in the *not pictured* section.

I remembered my yearbook being full of quotes from almost the whole school. My book had so many comments from friends saying "have a good summer" and "keep in touch." *We all started at an early age, acting like we gave a shit about each other.* I didn't have a blank page at the back of my yearbook.

Jesse's yearbook did not look like my yearbook. Only a handful of people signed his yearbook.

Chapter 36

DONTAE LIVED IN the project homes of Greensboro, North Carolina. Not exactly the first place I had in mind to meet a potential suspect, but I must go where this case takes me. Nothing could stop me now. I'm too far in. I'm in far enough to feel the pain of what Jesse must have felt in his last days, so deep that it didn't even hurt.

When I drove on Spring Garden Road, I tried to imagine what Dontae would look like. I had no pictures of him, just information from the pool man. I drove apprehensively as the front-porch guys stared at me. These are people I don't understand. I know that there are some situations that force people to have this low-income, subsidized lifestyle, but it seemed most of these people didn't care to get out. They blamed someone else for their circumstances. When I saw their faces, I felt like they were looking for a handout from me, but that wasn't all they wanted. They also wanted me to show some kind of guilt. They were disgusted and hated those people who had nicer living situations; and they expected us to feel sorry for them.

I know I am being short-sighted when I say that they put themselves there and they all had the power to get themselves out. Some, like the children, didn't have any control over their family's income.

Those that tried could still get out of this lifestyle. *There is no such thing as fate.* No one had a plan for them to be there. They put themselves there, whether it was by drugs, alcohol, or an inability to hold a steady job. It was their fault.

Those kids looked sad all the time. They have no structure in their behavior. They have no morals. Those kids deserve better than their druggy teenaged mom and dad. Unfortunately, now more than ever, it's a continuous life cycle for these people. Some will never get out of their current situation. Some only dream of getting out. Most would die here. *How could Jesse, a wealthy spoiled child, be friends with someone from a place like this? Was Dontae an outlier?*

Basketball was something that people of all socioeconomic backgrounds could enjoy. Georgio said they played basketball together, but he also said that they were very close. *How close? What was their connection other than basketball?*

I looked for the address and found it difficult since there were no numbers on most of the houses. That place reminded me of Spain in a way. Minus the property values and the overall dirt-poor neighborhood, all of the houses were similar. They all had the same front porch but with different old people sitting on the rocking chairs. Each house had windows exactly the same distance away from each other as the houses next to them. All three feet of the yards were trimmed perfectly to look as neat as possible. If you took away all of the people and the part of town this neighborhood was in, you could say that this was a pretty clean neighborhood.

I felt like I was devaluing myself by driving through that neighborhood. When I finally found the house, I questioned whether I should get out of the car. I took a deep breath, but it wasn't like the others.

I was here to find information about his relationship with Dontae. *What happened to their communication as they grew older? What happened on the night of the wreck?*

I strolled up to the house, nervously locking the car doors behind me. I felt people were staring at me, and they were moving in closer and closer. My greatest concern was the safety of the valuable information I had so far. It would be lost if I was robbed and murdered. I no longer feared my death but the death of information I had attained. I checked to see my surroundings through the bubble reflections in my driver's window. I needed this to go quickly. Even though it wasn't dark yet, I was scared as hell.

I walked down the beaten path and up their three steps to their front porch. *There was a stench of some kind coming out of the doorway. It was very strong and smelled almost like a skunk had been inside.* I decided it was not horrific enough to make me turn around, so I knocked on the door. I heard what seemed like a thousand children's footsteps running to the door, jumping up and down to see out of the peephole.

Then, I cringed at the sound of a scream.

"Stop jumping! Get your ass back to your room and shut the hell up!"

I wasn't familiar with this style of raising children, but I'm sure there are other effective ways to discipline your children. I knew I should not judge though. I had never had kids, and I wouldn't even know the basics of raising a child.

I had to snap out of this judgmental mentality. I needed the help of the woman behind the door. I needed her to let me in her house so I could find Dontae.

"Hello. How are you doing?" I said nervously. I felt as if she had an itchy trigger finger ready to blow me away.

"What do you want?"

Straight to the point but a little scary since she hadn't opened the door yet and might have a shotgun pointed at my gut right now.

"I already served my time. What do you want from me?"

"Ma'am, I'm here to see—"

"Don't ma'am me. Tell me what the hell you want. If you are

trying to serve Rebecca Smith you have the wrong house."

Who is Rebecca Smith? She wasn't letting me speak.

"I don't know who Rebecca Smith is, ma'am. I'm just looking for Dontae."

She was about to say something, and then she slammed her hands on the door. She hit it so hard that the physical pain was nowhere near the ocean of agony she had when I said his name. I could feel the agony she had through the door, but I also felt a relief because I finally found the lead I'd been looking for in my case. *Did Dontae run away? Was she ashamed of him? What would make this woman break down like that?* Obviously, she was close to him. She seemed to have an association with him that was deep, and now he was gone. Perhaps she had not talked to or seen Dontae in years. *Where did he go after the accident?* I knocked on the door again.

"Ma'am, I think you are misunderstanding why I am here."

No response. I hoped she was listening.

I tried my very best to stay and wait it out. All I wanted was a finger to point me in the right direction. *Just point, please.*

Chapter 37

"I AM AN investigator in Jesse Saunders murder. Jesse was good friends with Dontae, and I just need some background information on their relationship. Please, if you can help me, let me know." That was my final attempt at getting information from this emotionally disturbed woman.

Just as I turned to escape this dreadful place without the information I needed, the woman opened the door. I smelled a very distinct wind that I have never witnessed before. I walked a couple steps in the doorway so I could dodge the slamming door if she wished to speak with me no longer about Dontae's whereabouts.

"I'm Dontae's aunt. You can find Dontae downtown."

Great, I had my pointing finger. Now, it was time to gather as much information as I could to locate exactly where he was in order to move forward with this investigation.

"Great. I thought that he might be dead from the car accident he was in with Jesse."

I breathed a sigh of relief, only to see her face was showing that my presumption was correct.

"He is dead."

Goddamn it. There weren't supposed to be any lose-ends to this case.

Georgio was hiding something. He was sending me on a wild-goose chase so he could leave town.

"I'm sorry."

I tempered my frustration for coming to this terrible part of the city.

"He's dead to the world and dead to me. He had a great opportunity to make a difference in our family. First one to graduate high school, first one to college, first one to never be suspended for fighting, and more importantly the first one that wasn't addicted to crack cocaine."

I was already one foot out of the door, ready to face the fact that I had been working on something for days and it turned out to be a dud.

I still had to be polite because she did let me in and she didn't shoot me.

"I'm sorry for your loss, ma'am. I didn't know."

I wonder if she really thought I was sorry, because I truthfully was not. I don't know Dontae; how could I feel sorry for her loss? People that I don't know die every day. At least she was nice enough to tell me he was dead.

"You ain't no cop or DEA … are you?"

"No ma'am. Why do you ask?" I felt like Abby's burst of frustration was going to come out in this woman's voice. I had a talent for making people angry.

"Usually they can smell the coke cooking in the kitchen or the bags of hash on the counter."

I pushed back the thought of her becoming angry and began to listen to what she was saying. She was telling me the truth. *But what if I was a cop? Did she let me in so she could kill me? Could I have made a run to my car before she got a gun? I was so confused.* Maybe it was because I was becoming more like Jesse, an easygoing and accepting person. I had a friendly smile and genuinely cared for people. *There's also the possibility that it was just because I was alone and white.*

"But anyway, you can find Dontae on the second floor in the downtown jail; cell block C. You gonna' need this pass to get to the upper levels and make sure you take off anything that could be considered a weapon. I damn near got locked up for having a sharp chopstick holdin' my weave up." I was almost smiling for the first time in weeks. This change of events bolstered the confidence I almost lost in Jesse's case.

"If you don't mind me asking, why is he in jail?"

"Why does anyone living in this neighborhood go to jail? He's in jail for drugs."

"I thought he was above that?"

"He didn't do drugs. He just sold them with his father. He got caught in one them sting operations they do … on Greene Street."

This new information gave me a clear understanding about why Jesse had not remained friends with Dontae. If his parents knew about Dontae's drug dealing, they would have told him that he had to find new friends. *But Georgio said Jesse's friends were good kids.*

"How close were Dontae and Jesse?"

"Well, they were like shadows of one another. They would hang out and play ball every day. There wasn't a day of summer that Jesse and Dontae didn't play eight hours of ball at the park. The park is right down yonder … to your right off of Elam. But don't take a left, you hear?"

"Jesse had a little bit of a struggle fitting into the crowd at first, but he eventually became chill with the people down there. They called him little white flea. But he liked it. Jesse was so white and so fast that people couldn't guard him. It was a perfect nickname for him. Plus, if you didn't have a nickname from here, you didn't belong here. Jesse was something else, you know that? I have never seen a bunch of juiced up guys in their thirties let two sixteen-year-olds play ball with them, especially if one of the kids was white and rich."

"Well, all of this information is greatly appreciated, and I am starting to piece this together."

I recalled her reaction to hearing about Jesse's murder. *She didn't show any remorse for Jesse's death.* I was becoming too good at my job. I suspected everyone for murder. *Maybe she was so used to death that it became a natural thing for her.* She was probably more concerned about me being an officer and locking her up again.

As I walked out it felt like I had Jesse's presence here in this awful place. I felt confident that no one would hurt me here. I walked back to the car, waved goodbye to a door that was already closed and felt relief that something was going my way. This was the reason I had to do this investigation. I had to find out things about Jesse's past and work my way toward the day he died to make sure I got the full concept of what I was trying to accomplish. I had to prove *them* wrong.

Chapter 38

DONTAE COULD OBVIOUSLY not be a suspect for the murder directly, but I have come to realize that anyone could've killed Jesse, even if they weren't there when he died.

He was in jail. Jail was a place I would rather not visit again. I hated that place, and it was sad that I knew my way around it. Not because I was a frequent visitor, but because I was just here recently.

I parked in the parking garage and made my way to the police station. I didn't know exactly the procedure to get up to the second floor of this place, but I had residual confidence from earlier to find my way without feeling like I wanted to leave. The police station had a way of making you feel like you were in big-time trouble just by walking up the stairs to the front door. The marble steps were a reminder that all of those freedoms we took for granted would be absent inside the cell. There are no marble steps to your cell. Just cement and a hairy roommate who will probably want sexual favors as you got to know each other.

I started to think about those guys staring at me when I was driving down Dontae's neighborhood street. Those guys would probably live a better life in here. They would have free food and a warm, clean place to stay. Of course, sexual needs would not be met unless heterosexuality was no longer important. If they had females in jail, it would be the perfect place for anyone living in poverty. It would be like a paradise for them. Jesse always talked about where our taxes go, and I never really listened until he said something about us providing the poor with a home and food when we, the free people, could barely feed ourselves anymore.

I walked into the building feeling a strong gust of wind blowing from the air-conditioning unit pressing down on me. Immediately past the strong air flow, I was checked for guns, weapons, and other incriminating objects. I don't exactly remember where I was taken when I was here before, but this place felt familiar.

The person across the window at the desk asked me where I was going and what department I was seeing.

"Second floor, please. I have a visitation pass here."

I should have thanked Dontae's aunt more for this information and the pass. She was surprisingly kind after I reached through her barricade of emotions.

She pointed and said, "Down the hall, take a right … stop at the counter … and use the elevator."

"Thank you." I took a look at her name tag because names are so important. "Jamie."

I walked down the hallway, listening to each step echo off of the walls like water dripping into a can. I approached the next counter where the desk officer had another guard pat me down for drugs and weapons. There was a loud sound that only silenced after I opened and closed the door. The sound of an alarm with no warning from either one of the guards pierced my eardrum and sent vibrations into the frontal lobe of my brain. *What the hell!*

I pressed two on the elevator, still wondering what Dontae looked like. *I wondered if he was a gangster-looking guy. Maybe he is one of those guys who were in the wrong place at the wrong time.* From his aunt's story, that sounded like a probable explanation.

I went to the room where Dontae was waiting for me. Although I didn't know what he looked like, when I walked into the room, I knew it was him. Not because he was the only one at a table alone, but because he looked up at me with assurance. He had no idea who I was or what I was doing there, but I knew it was him and he knew it was me. *I hope he doesn't think I'm a lawyer or somebody to help get him out of this dump.*

"Dontae?" It was as if I did not have to question myself anymore, as he was cleaning off the table and pulling up a chair for me.

"Yes sir." *Wrong place at the wrong time.*

"Hello. I'm here to talk to you about your relationship with Jesse."

He had a certain look about him, a look of defeat. He must have been a tagalong in this drug bust. He didn't seem like a leader of such crimes. I was analyzing his words, the way he talked, and the way he carried himself. He was educated. He was smart enough to get out of the place he was living in. She was right. He wasn't a lost cause like everyone else in his neighborhood; he had somewhere to go in life. *Jesse had an extreme strength of will. He helped Dontae. Jesse had a way of motivating and piercing people with enthusiasm.*

"Okay. Well, he used to be one of my best friends. We played ball together every day when we were kids. We worked on specific skills all of the time, even in high school when we did not play for the same team anymore. During the summers we were always playing at the park with the other adults, when we were good enough."

"So I'm guessing you guys played basketball every time you were together?"

"Yeah, we did. We were going to play college ball together. He always used to tell me that I was going to get a college scholarship at the same school he was at." Jesse's optimism was infective. He spread the infection of having dreams and aspirations. "He had these crazy ideas about us making it big in the pros, too."

"So you are younger than him?"

"No." Dontae spoke faster than before, as if he were ashamed, "I was in tenth grade twice."

He already answered half of the questions I had in the first two minutes. I liked this guy.

"Oh, okay. I found an old yearbook of his and that's how I found your information. I was wondering where your picture was in the yearbook because I saw your address and phone number on the back of the book, but I couldn't find your class picture."

"I went to Southside Andrews, and his parents moved him to Northern High. We didn't play each other school v. school. Even though that would have been pretty cool. We never saw any of each other's games because my school was playing the same nights as his school. I'm pretty sure his school was smaller than mine too."

"Thanks for clearing that up."

"No problem, isn't that what we're here for?" I was relieved he didn't think I had the ability to get him out of here.

"Yes sir. What happened to your friendship after high school?"

"Well, he got cut his senior year of basketball. He had a lot of things happen to him that year."

He was thinking about his next statement. I was thinking that was all he was going to say about his relationship with Jesse.

"If you don't mind me asking, how did you end up here?"

"Well, it all started with Jesse and me deciding where we were going to play ball. He always came over to my house so we could play ball at the park. Jesse had a car, so he could get here to play. One day he asked if I wanted to play ball at his place instead."

I nodded my head. "Uh huh."

"I remember his driveway was bigger than three of my houses. But anyway, we were playing ball later than usual, probably like eight or nine o'clock at night. The plan was to play ball all day, and I was going to sleep over at his house. I remember being really excited about that since he had so many rooms. I could actually sleep in my own room with my own bed. I can't tell you enough what close friends we were. We were like brothers, man. I kind of had this hope when I was younger that his parents would adopt me."

I saw his eyes tear up. He had nothing before; no emotion. When he remembered the time he lost his best friend, his brother, he slowly dissolved the tough image he was trying to maintain.

"Then something happened while he was in another room talking to his parents. He came out and slammed the door. I have never seen Jesse angry before. He told me to get into the car. I didn't say anything until we got down the road. I asked him what was wrong, and he said, 'Someone in the family died, and I need to take you home.'"

"Do you know who died?" I was curious to know why he would be angry about someone dying in his family.

"I was so used to people dying in my neighborhood that it really didn't even affect me anymore. When I was five I witnessed my mom being murdered over drugs. But he was sad and angry at the same time. He began to speed. He would usually just speed up to the speed limit and then he would slow down. Just to show off his car a little bit. His car was really fast. He always told me what his father said to him when they bought the car. 'If we buy this car, you have to promise me that you won't wrap it around a tree.' It's a little ironic, looking back now."

"I remembered my sixteen-year-old days," I said. "I drove my father's Porsche on the weekends, speeding up and down the roads like a cocky asshole." He grinned a little. His protective wall returned so I knew I was about to hear something important.

"But this time he kept going. We must have been doing like seventy miles per hour on a neighborhood road. Then it happened. I saw the stop sign … but my aunt always told me, 'You never tell anyone how to drive their own car.'"

I could relate to this quote because my mom said the same thing. I used to point out when she was going faster than the speed limit.

She always covered up the speedometer and said, "When you have a driver's license and a car of your own, then you can tell me how to drive."

"… So I didn't tell him that he needed to slow down for the stop sign. We hit the other car nearly head-on. We were both knocked unconscious and came to at the same time. I couldn't remember anything. We heard the squealing tires of someone coming up beside us. There was glass everywhere. I heard Jesse saying, 'No. No, this isn't really happening. I need to wake up.'"

"I will always remember what he said, and I was kind of hoping he was right. I couldn't speak when it happened. He glanced over at me with a bloody face to make sure I was still breathing. Neither one of us could move. We just looked up through the windshield at the hood of his car crushed upward past the line of sight."

He started to struggle with his words. He probably hadn't told anyone about this part of the story.

"I got out of the car on my hands and knees. My ears were ringing so I couldn't hear a thing. Glass was everywhere; on the street, in my hair, in the seats, the carpet, and in my skin. I was bleeding so much. Jesse got out of the car and started screaming for help. Bystanders just looked at us like we were just a bunch of kids racing cars. They didn't help us. Jesse went over to the car we hit. It was an older lady. She was bleeding too. She looked like she was hyperventilating. I remember this part of the evening changed Jesse. He was screaming, 'Someone help please! God! Get someone over here. HELP! Oh God please help her! Pleaseeeeee!' I couldn't do anything but sit down and think about how lucky we all were. Then I thought about the stop sign. I didn't know if he could see it or not. I felt partially responsible for that night. He had to have known about the stop sign. He must have known that I saw it and didn't say anything. I just know that's why we were never like we were before."

Fatalism begins with an unexpected event to a vulnerable person.

Chapter 39

"So what happened to your relationship after that?"

"Well, we hung out a couple days after, and he initially said that the lady looked like she was going to recover from her injuries. So I was happy to hear that. Then the next thing he told me was the last thing he ever told me, 'I can't play ball with you anymore. I can't come over to your place. I can't even speak to you anymore. I don't want to be your friend and I don't want anything to do with you.' How was I supposed to respond to my best friend who just said that? My brother ... He was like family to me. It almost sounded like someone else was saying the words through him. I don't have any connections with him or basketball anymore. That's when my life started going downhill. That's why I'm here. He kept me away from all of that shit. Last I heard he had a teaching certificate from a college in Greensboro. What do you know about him?"

"Well, I am investigating his death." I was wondering how he would take this news. His aunt showed nothing and seemed to think the world of him, but Dontae had a different reaction.

"Jesse is dead? How did he die? When did it happen?" *This concern from Dontae was intriguing. He said he was used to death, but*

was this a cover-up? I couldn't stop thinking that this concern was a
sham in order for him to appear innocent.

"He was murdered about two weeks ago."

"Has anyone been convicted yet?"

"No sir … but there is a list of suspects. Basically what I'm trying
to do is to gather all of the information that I can about Jesse before
I make a conviction. Now, the lady you were talking about, the one
that he crashed into, where can I find her?"

I was playing off this Alex Cross detective talk now. I wanted to
be a detective of the law for just this one case. This was too personal
to be just a normal FBI case.

Chapter 40

"Guess I left that part out. I found out later on in that year, from my friend Marquett that the lady died. She died from blood loss and a collapsed lung."

He spoke with such normalcy. It was something I wasn't used to in my life.

"Was it from the accident?"

"Yeah … she died in the hospital about four days after it happened. Marquett told me Jesse was being charged with vehicular manslaughter, and the police came to his work to serve him."

That's what happened at the pool. *Georgio was right. He told the truth. I allowed myself to like Georgio now. I was waiting for him to be in the clear. He and Abby were the only suspects I wanted to be innocent.*

"So that's how the Dontae and Jesse story ends, huh?"

I exhaled a slight chuckle because everything Dontae told me about Jesse made sense. This story was starting to come together for me. Once I had everything documented and I had the proof, I was going to show *them* what they overlooked.

"Pretty much."

"Well, thank you for your time and I hope the best for you

in here."

"Good luck."

I added another crime to the list of Jesse's parents' charges. They were responsible for that woman's death. They were responsible for Jesse driving while emotionally charged. *There was no family member who passed away.* There were just two judgmental white parents who didn't want a black person to sleep over in their house. That was the reason Jesse was driving erratically. He wasn't himself. The parents are to blame for the vehicular manslaughter, and I had the proof.

Chapter 41

"HAVE YOU TALKED to him yet? Are you guys still going out?" She was as excited as I was about that night.

It was the first time he had said yes to one of my open invitations to something more social than his girlfriend's sorority formals.

"Yes, Mom. He said he was. I don't think his girlfriend likes me though."

"Well, she only needs time to get to know you, dear." She was always so confident in me. Even after I had been in college for six years and was finally graduating.

"I know. We'll have fun tonight. It's going to be his early birthday party."

"Okay, you be careful now. Sounds like you two are finally getting to know each other. I am happy for you guys, but please be careful."

I always heard her say careful before saying good-bye. I was always careful. Careful enough.

"Okay, I love you, bye."

The irony of dying on his birthday.

Part IV

ILLEK

I FELT SO much better about the investigation. I had new incriminating evidence I just found from the suspects. I put together piece by piece exactly what the suspects said about Jesse's life in my head. I needed to spend some time putting all of the evidence on paper to start my proposal for justice.

I walked up my apartment steps and wondered if Jesse would have ever landed the teaching job he desired. *Would that have prevented them from murdering him?* There was something I needed to still find out. I needed more than what I had to make my decision. I was more ready than ever for what lay ahead than I have ever felt before. Nothing was going to stop this from happening.

When I walked into our room, I had a letter on my desk that came from the murder scene. It was unopened, and I was very interested about what could be inside. It could be a letter from Professor Bea saying that he didn't finish his credits to graduate school. It could be a confession of love for him by his ex-girlfriend Abby. *It could say, "Jesse I have made a mistake by leaving you. I miss you dearly and I am coming back to the states." Maybe it was a post-murder letter.* It could be someone saying I love you, when they either forgot or had never said it to him before. *Maybe it was a*

confession from Mom and Dad saying it was their fault he died.
Instead it was a letter that read:

Jesse,

We appreciate your interest in our school. There were a large number of qualified applicants for this position. At this time we have chosen another candidate for the position. Please continue to check with us for opportunities in the future. Thank you for your time and energy and may peace be with you.

Best regards,
Gary Goldberg

There were a lot of similar short letters from schools who had rejected him. *Why couldn't they see what everyone else saw in him?* He would give them his heart, and he would volunteer more time than they would ever need him to, as a teacher. He had s*o much to give and nowhere to give it.* I wondered if he would've gotten a teaching job if he had lived.

It seemed like no one was giving him a chance. No one was seeing the true Jesse. I remembered him telling me a story about job interviews and job offers. He told me that the school where he had finished his student teaching was going to hire him if the teacher retired, like she said she was going to do. She didn't retire, and Jesse didn't start looking for a job until after he found out the news. He told me, "I got to tell you something, man. Never ever put all your eggs in one basket even if there is an almost guarantee of them hatching." He was very upset when he found out, but somehow he kept his smile that we saw every day. The school where he did his student teaching was a great school, and it would have started a very bright future for him in the world of education. He had put all of his hopes into that school. *I wondered if he had given up in those interviews at other schools.*

He told me, "If you want something that bad, you better put everything you have into it happening. I thought it was a given I would get the job, and I took it for granted. I should have had a backup plan. I should have had a failsafe. I needed something concrete. This whole summer I have been working with nothing but maybe, possibly, and perhaps. Find a concrete job and use it as a plan in case your first plan fails." He gave me good advice all of the time. I only listened to some of it.

I admit that he rubbed off on me like everyone else with whom he had contact. I became an honest person around him because someone like him deserved the truth. He made it safe for us to speak the truth about things with him, the truth we all hide behind.

Journal Entry

I thought it would be a good idea to see what it was like, joining a fraternity. I also accepted the fact that she would not leave the sorority she joined. Why did she join a sorority? We were so good together before she did that. She probably was influenced by one of those fraternity mattress girls. Those girls didn't know anything about a relationship.

I know I should leave her, but I'm so comfortable with her. I won't leave her. I feel if I can't win, I could join her. For her, I was going to sell myself out. Everything I stood against my whole college life was getting ready to be violated for her.

One of my college friends joined a fraternity, and he was still my good friend. I looked up to him because he was older. He brought me to a party last night at their fraternity house, and all of his fraternity brothers were really nice to me. I am not used to a bunch of people coming up to me and acting like they liked me. They gave me all of the free beer I could imagine. It was a good feeling to feel important. I didn't drink a whole lot because I had my guard up, ready for one foolish brother with a stupid paddle, expecting him to hit me. This Greek gathering was the first one I had gone to, and she was with me. It made her happy for me to go there. I thought it might be actually okay to see this thing through.

We were drinking at a table and talking when one of the guys came running up from downstairs saying, "Where's Jesse Saunders?" I thought about running because they weren't going to demoralize me. I wasn't going to get spanked in front of all these people. I told Illek to leave, but her eyes held me back. They told me to sit down. Somehow I trusted her even when I knew that whatever was going to happen, it wasn't going to be enjoyable.

When he found me he said I had to come upstairs. I was very weary of my surroundings. Not because the house was ready to fall apart, but because none of the brothers were downstairs, just me and another guy and about twenty women. We walked upstairs. The other guy seemed to know what was going on, and he was really excited. All of the girls were cheering us on. I didn't know what this meant. All I could think about was, were they getting ready to rape us? I'd heard rumors about this fraternity.

Upstairs I saw the strangest thing I have ever seen in my entire life. I saw hooded men and only heard their voices. I didn't see their faces. They started speaking from a script that sounded like Old English. I started looking for an escape, but the hooded brothers surrounded us. The other guy was called up to the front where the leader of this hooded group asked him a question. "Do you want twenty-four hours, or do you want to accept right now?" He said, "Right now!" The loud cheer from the group inside the room caused the girls downstairs to renew their applause. Then it was my turn. I decided to say the same thing as the guy before because I was uncertain about what would happen if I chose the twenty-four hours instead. I accepted their offer when I really didn't know what it meant, until now.

The next day she woke me up exactly the way I love to be woken up. I it feels so good because it's so unexpected and warm. I liked making her happy. She told me that she was proud of me. What was she proud about? Was it because I said right now instead of 24 hours? That seemed an easy thing to do to make her happy. I didn't voice my concerns about it because I didn't want her to get upset. I always have to be careful when she's happy because it's like everything I said started to dance on her eggshells of happiness. One word could smash this good thing we had going now.

Because of the events of last night I had to go to a meeting. Apparently I accepted a bid for their fraternity. I am a pledge and a bid holder. They told us that we should feel honored because there were only a certain amount of bids given out each semester.

Then they brought the paddle out for the pledges. I can still feel how the blood rushed to my face. One by one they were lining up to get paddled. The other pledge from last night looked at me and said, "Looks like we're going to be pledge brothers, man. You got to do what you got to do to be a Kappa Delta Row!" How pathetic these people were. I didn't stand up. My friend looked at me and motioned his shoulders to tell me to stand up, but I didn't. I wasn't going to lose myself just to make her happy. I had to stand up for myself. They said, "Jesse, if you want to be a part of this, then you need come here." I wouldn't stand. "Jesse, come on man!" I felt bad because he told them to let me into their private party. I knew that I was going to feel bad for saying what I was about to say if they kept egging me on. "Jesse," they said and I blew up. I told them, "No. I will not stand for this. I will not be your pledge. I will not be slapped with a paddle. I'm sorry. My father did that enough when I was younger." I started to leave, but these guys thought that I must have been joking. They stepped in front of the door, grabbed my arm and said, "That's two for you now, boy." I was angry. I shrugged them off and gave them a shove. "No, screw that, and screw you too!"

I had enough true friends. I didn't need this fraternity. Screw them. Illek was angry at me, but I had kept my dignity. She'll be better. I hope."

Chapter 42

I READ HIS journal about my fraternity, and I thought if he would have joined the fraternity, he would have been categorized and isolated. I know he didn't have a lot of friends, but the friends he had were as good as five of my fraternity brothers. *But maybe a fraternity is what he needed. Maybe he needed to have that brotherhood in his life. I just thought that he was missing true friends here in college.*

I usually put aside my love for my fraternity to keep him interested in becoming my friend. It didn't bother me to join in on his jokes. In fact, I made a couple of my own.

In Jesse's journal, he mentioned that people who joined these fraternities make a ton of paid friends and forget about their true friends that they had for free. *How could you lose a true friend?* Your true friends should stay with you until the end and through the tough and good times. *I agreed with most of his words about the Kappa Delta Row fraternity except for that part. What if he really needed that brotherly love my fraternity guys shared together? What if all the people who knew him would've made the same effort, to really understand someone, like Jesse did?*

His girlfriend at the time of the murder was in a sorority. I remembered seeing Jesse upset about her joining a sorority. His

155

journal proved that he never truly got over the fact that she joined a sorority. True, he tried to cope with it, but his attempt failed. He would always argue with her about how it was a tremendous waste of money and how he could help her find better friends than any one of those girls in the group could. He always got worked up about it whenever the subject came up in conversation. *That was the one thing that even Saint Jesse couldn't just brush off his shoulder.*

His girlfriend for the last two and a half years was Illek. Illek was someone he had an instant attraction to, and she lit up the room for him wherever he was in the world. He was truly in love. He was probably just as in love with Illek as he had been with Abby. He didn't even look at other girls the same. Other girls he encountered had no chance of becoming anything more than just a friend acquaintance.

He was so dedicated in keeping the relationship for the long term. She was his world, and she could do no wrong in his book. Until she decided to join a sorority and became a person he didn't want her to become.

Why did this upset him so much? These were the questions I wanted to find out from my meeting with her. I heard she easily got a temper in all kinds of situations. I wondered if she could go from happy to sad as fast as Abby went from sorrow to anger. I am guessing she could, since I have seen her lose it in one out of the three times I have met her.

Chapter 43

NONE OF JESSE'S friends, including me, liked Illek. She was not the best at first impressions. But since this investigation, neither was I. Jesse told me that Illek didn't like people at all. She shut herself off from others when they were together. It was like she didn't want to like anyone besides him. He once told me, "She didn't even like some of the friends she'd paid for."

I had only met her a couple of times before *that* night. She knows, and should feel some sort of responsibility for what happened to Jesse that night. She was the reason we got caught that night. I noticed that it was never anything she said, but more of the way she said it and how she acted disgusted all the time. She came across as an angry person. *Angry at the world, I guess.*

They were polar opposites. I imagine he walked out on her every time she yelled at him because he didn't want to say something that would hurt their relationship. *What did he see in her?*

Don't get me wrong. Jesse never felt like she wasn't the right person to take home to meet Mom and Dad, because she definitely qualified for him. She was graduating at the same time as him with a nursing degree. Her salary would've supplemented Jesse's teaching salary. Jesse's mom and dad always worried about his salary. They

157

couldn't understand why he didn't become a business major like his father or go into the engineering program like his mother.

He could never be fully accepted by his parents, it seemed. I worried about my investigation because as I thought about any situation, I always fell to blaming his parents for this crime. *They were just so easy to blame.*

Illek lived in an apartment near the school. She had gone through eight different roommates in two years. That should have been a sign for Jesse. *If he was going to spend the rest of his life with her, would he be wanting to move out all of the time, like all of her old roommates?*

Illek held onto everything. She never let anything go because it bothered her so much. Whether it was the dishes, the trash, the dog's accidents, or just roommate drama, everything was worth arguing over to her. She was never satisfied and never content with the way something was, no matter what.

Chapter 44

I CAME TO her apartment. It was a townhome with two levels. She lived at 2011 Sherwood Complex. I thought it was funny that her address was the same as the year the Americans took back Ground Zero from the Muslims.

I saw her car and I felt relief that she was here. Something had to be accomplished in this interview before I started to doubt this whole process. I took my deep breath. I have thought long and deep about this interrogation with Illek ever since I got back from Spain.

How did Jesse do this to himself? It was killing my will to live and I did not think I'd ever adjust to that. I had some things I wanted to clear up, but I had to be careful with her because I needed her testimony.

I knocked on her door. I did not know what to expect, but what I saw amazed me. Her facial structure was perfect. Her green eyes must be the prettiest body part I have ever seen on a female. I could lose myself in her eyes. She had a tan complexion like Abby, but I knew that it was a fake tan. Abby had a natural-looking tan that brought up no question as to whether it was real or not. Illek went to the tanning bed, probably every day. Even with the fake tan, her body was something I could never forget. I wanted to see her naked in front of me. She was very curvy and not too skinny. She was wearing a blue dress that fit her well. She also had a wonderful smile.

"Hel—" I interrupted her before she could finish.

"Please ... let's get right to it." I wasn't exactly starting off on the right foot as I made my demand. I saw that I was already pissing her off by interrupting, because her upper facial muscles dropped midway through my sentence.

"Okay ... I see you only came here for one reason, so let's get to it."

Making her comfortable again was going to be a task. I knew by the way she responded. I just wanted to be able to either blame her for his murder or mark her name off the list.

I could almost taste the selfishness in her voice. *How could he love her? How could anyone ever love her? Was it just because she had a pretty face that reminded him of Abby?* She wasn't worth his time.

Her face was a lever ... the anger in her forehead muscles unclenched their downward wrinkles and rotated up, while at the same time her jawbone lowered with concern. She took a few rushed steps toward me.

"You're bleeding! Here, put this on it and press down hard. Keep your arm above your head." She must be good at whatever she did in the nursing department. It was evident by how resourceful she was.

"I can't find the origin of this. What did you slice yourself on?"

Then it hit me. I knew why Jesse loved her.

I did not know where or why I was bleeding. I just knew that her attention to my injury was her way of showing affection. She had love for people. *Why does she say she hates people?* She wanted to help people who were hurt. She had the ability to love, a medical romance.

I wondered if any of his friends were hurt and she helped them.

If they saw her love for helping sick or injured people, they would like her too. I was already beginning to enjoy her company just by the mere decency of her bandaging a wound for me. She made me feel comfortable again. I almost allowed my body to rest, but then I snapped back out of it, remembering why I was here.

Jesse loved her because of the mothering she performed in her nursing. She was really good at making me feel relaxed as she took care of me.

I remembered a time where Jesse was very sick. A common cold mixed with his asthma might have been a deadly combination. He could barely eat or drink anything because of a sore throat. He could barely drink a small Gatorade without it taking ten minutes because it hurt him to swallow. Illek was at the house every day to take care of him. *I remember so many times telling him to stop being a bitch and take the pain like a man. I regret saying that, especially since I could barely take his pain.*

It took Jesse two weeks to recover. I don't think he could have survived as well as he did without her. She cared for him so much that he knew that he was going to spend the rest of his life with her. There was no doubt in my mind that her caring was the reason he fell in love. She was the one because she cared about his well-being. She had the soft side for helping people, but like a rose, she had plenty of thorns preventing anyone new from approaching.

They went through their ups and downs like any other relationship, except for the fact that she was always the person being walked out on because she had that Texas Pete temper. I would hear her yelling at him in his own apartment, and he was the one who left to get away from her every time. I hated when Jesse did that because it was always awkward when it was just her and me in the apartment. I always pretended I didn't hear her cry. I would stay as far away from her as possible.

Journal Entry

She did it again. She screamed at me. The replacement of one word kills me. It used to say love in this three-word phrase. She replaced it with the only word that could hurt me the most. She didn't understand why I didn't finish what I started with the fraternity. <u>*I didn't know what I was starting! How does something like dropping a fraternity, make someone say they hate you?*</u>

I only knew one way to make her come back to me. I've only done it a few times before, but this I was going to do it with her in the other room. I wanted her to hear me in pain. I wanted her to come in and save me. I added new lines for every minute that passed. For a second, I thought to myself that she might not come to help me. I was really scared, but for some unexplainable reason, for the first time, I started to laugh while I did it. I laughed because I thought that I might run out of places. My skin was on the run.

I locked myself in her bathroom and did it over and over. It was painful, being with her. She cared so much about my body; well, she cared so much about people's bodies. She wanted everyone's body to be healthy. She wanted to help everybody, but she didn't know what it meant to take care of someone's emotions because she didn't take care of herself. She was a mess, a total wreck. She knew how to be

163

happy, but she didn't have the tools to continue that emotion for longer than the time it took to stop the bleeding. I did it again and I'm not proud.

She started crying tears of frustration, lacking any type of control. Sobbing and sulking at the thought of me being physically hurt, she realized she couldn't help me. This was the only thing I could do that she had no control over. Persuading her to do something she didn't want was impossible. She never wanted to take a step out of her comfort zone. I know I'm not the best at breaking out of my shell, but she was terminally inflexible. She's like my stubborn skin. I had control over her with only this one curse. Why couldn't it be something else? I liked this change of scenery. I didn't want her to be easy enough to pierce right through both sides of her. But she could keep her basic personality and still have the ability to enter through the skin to see her true feelings. I wanted her to bleed with me. I wanted it to be easier to be with her. This habit wouldn't have been my first choice, but it worked. It was like a successful play in football. Why would you stop doing the same play? Keep on using that play until it doesn't work anymore.

I mark my words on this paper, "Illek, I love you, but you're trying to force me to do something I don't want to do. I can't do what you want me to do. I don't want to make a list with the things that I don't like about you, but your jealousy over someone who is hundreds of miles away is annoying me." She said nothing. She didn't admit, apologize or show in any way that she was sorry. She just hugged me. It's not like I've never received a hug from her before, it's just that she doesn't normally make gestures like that. I loved her when she was like this, and I'll do whatever it takes to make her come back to me.

Illek almost has a right to be jealous over her. Whenever Illek went on one of her temper tantrums I thought about her. She was the love of my life. I have to stop thinking about her because she was no longer here. She is far away from me. I wanted to go find her and escape the lie I was living <u>again.</u> She could save me again, like she did before. <u>But she didn't tell me where she was going.</u> I missed her and I know that's why I didn't have patience with Illek anymore. It was so easy to be with <u>her.</u> She was the one for me, and the frustration of not being able to have her was shattering my relationship with Illek.

My idol, Jesse Lacey said, "Some men die under the mountain just looking for gold; some die looking for a hand to hold." I was always looking for her hand to hold. I wanted an unconditional love unlike that of my parents. I wanted something wonderful. I wanted her to be like she was when she came into the bathroom and sat down next to me. I wanted her attention, her love, her sexual drive to stay with me. I didn't have to have this all of the time, but when I did, that's the moment I would realize that I have the woman of my dreams right here in front of me. Everything's okay if you settle enough.

She kissed me all over to stop the tears from coming down my face. Her love lifted me up to her bed. We made love the best after I went through my new habit. Sex was always the best way to heal, especially since I found a way to make her legs shake at the same time mine do. I love her.

Yesterday, my dad talked to me for the first time since they took me out of that place. It was the scariest thing that I have ever done. I never want to go back to that place. He asked me what the scabs were on my arms. My heart dropped because I knew he wanted to send me back. I almost thought I should tell him, but it would have been like the last time when I ran away.

This wasn't the first time I had done it. Now, I do it because it is the only way to make Illek surrender her anger towards me. It was different than all of the other times because before I wasn't asking for someone's help. Before, I just did it because it was the only getaway I had from my mom. And if there was ever a real restart button, I would have tried harder.

I hated that place they put me. The people in that place looked like they actually wanted to be there forever. They had this drugged-up happy feeling all of the time. The white coats gave me a pill that made me feel even more depressed. I wasn't sick and I hated hearing people telling me I was. Every day I would count down the days. I wasn't trying to kill myself, I would never do that, I just needed the escape it gave me. I tried to put on this happy face for everyone in there so they would let me out.

My parents sent me there because it was the easiest way for them to forget about me. Every day I spent in there, I wondered if they would ever come to visit. They never came. They never even came to the required intervention. What I hated most about that place was, even after several no-shows, they still put me in the visitation room. I had to sit there and listen to lies covering up the real reason my parents didn't show up. These employees were so used to their daily work tasks that they knew what to do in every situation. I watched them as they became bewildered with my case. They left me in the room alone with two empty chairs for hours. No one wanted to be the person to tell me they weren't coming. I don't like even thinking about that place. I wasn't going back there.

I quickly regained my confidence in my face and told him that I was playing rugby with Danny and the boys. He believed me. I think. This was the first time I lied to my father.

I had to hide myself from my own father. As if he wasn't hidden from me already. Since that day, my father hasn't spoken to me. He didn't understand nor did he want to hear any reasoning. I desperately wanted to see how my video game would end now. I still want my restart button, but I want to see how he would cope. If I saw him trying to cope with the loss of me, then maybe I could believe he loved me. I wonder if he would cry, get angry, become torn apart or even miss me when I was gone. I bet he wouldn't.

I don't know how long I can go on lying to my father, but my mother is another story. My mother has given me plenty of reasons to lie with no remorse. My father has always been a distant father.

Rarely ever showing his opinion on anything, his entire married life he has consistently been controlled by my mother's views. My mother directed both of our lives and my father wanted no confrontation, so he allowed this to happen, to both of us.

Chapter 45

"STAY WITH ME, you're going to be okay. Do you know what you cut yourself on? Have you had a tetanus shot recently?"

I felt the sincerity of her concern starting to fade into an act. I wanted her to stop pretending to care and show her true side. I noticed how Illek had gone from full resentment to caring so quickly. This changed my theory. People have different emotional ties. Different emotions bleed in on one another because they are not that far apart for most people. Some people seemed to display only one side, and they would drift too far; because of that, their other emotions would fade away from sight.

"Yes, I'm okay. This happens when I try to piece together my evidence and all of the things my suspects have said."

"But what did you cut yourself on?" The concerned face still surfaced on her skin. She wanted to help, and I could tell that she meant it.

"I don't know."

"Well, keep this on it." She handed me piece of gauze this time. I took it out of her hand and gave her the hint that I wanted to go inside by taking a step forward.

"Come in here. Do you need anything else? Water? Soda? Or

anything to help you relax?"

"No, I'm fine. Let's just get started." She could tell this whole scene was about to change.

"So what exactly did your message say to …"

"I want to know more about Jesse. I'm here to find out what really happened with him."

I saw that she wanted to cut into my next sentence. I spoke louder than she did to make my point that I was in charge of the direction this discussion was going to take.

"Well, I can tell you as much as you probably already know." We had a similar personality trait. We both get straight to the point with no filler.

"Tell me something about Jesse." I tilted my head down and took a serious look into her eyes. *Those eyes were set to kill. I could not afford to lose my train of thought during this interrogation.* "If you really knew Jesse, you would know …"

"Should we sit down first?"

I nodded my head and took the lead walking toward the stools. She had a bar set up that looked over the kitchen. I grabbed my seat and felt the pain of my arm flame up through the veins in my shoulders. *Damn that hurts.* I sat up on the stool and put my hurt arm on the counter. Being short, she struggled hopping up onto the stool, failing on her first attempt.

"Please." I made a scooping curve with my arm towards her indicating that I wanted her to continue when she was finally seated.

"Jesse was a man of principle, and whatever he thought was right, was right. Sometimes he would argue with me about joining a sorority. I always told him that being in a sorority for me was perfect, because I had no true friends or what he used to called them … free friends. He always referred to true friends as being free. I had to remind him that I used to have a boyfriend who isolated me from all of my friends, and I didn't want him to be that way with me. I never wanted him to give me the ultimatums like my old boyfriend Chris used to. Are you sure you're okay?"

"Yes, please carry on."

"You look kind of gray. Have you eaten recently? Do you feel nauseous? You should lay down." I was frustrated with her reluctance to continue, and it started to wear me down. I had to ask myself those questions because I couldn't remember. *Had I eaten? How long have I been up?* The answers were still a blur to me.

"I'm okay. I just haven't been able to rest."

"I know how you feel. This was a huge loss for me too. I can't even imagine how much pain this has brought you. You know I have gotten in fights with people who said those things about you. I told them all that it wasn't fair to say those things. I supported you." Although this was true, I didn't appreciate the recognition she desired for supporting me. She seemed to talk with such empathy, when she had no idea.

She didn't have a clue how much pain this case had brought to me. I have been struggling without support in this murder case since I started it. Everyone had given up on what happened. It was like everyone had forgotten already. They forgot Jesse but would never fail to blame me. I used to have a psychology professor who started his doctoral dissertation with testing the ability of people to forget. He said, to have the ability to make new long-term meaningful memories, we all needed to have the ability to forget. "It's like when you park your car in the parking garage. You try to remember where you parked today, but before you remember that, you need to forget where you parked yesterday." Before I spoke with the suspects and launched these interrogations, it was like people had already forgotten Jesse. *It's okay. They will see me soon and never forget what will happen.*

"It's quite all right. I will rest when this case is closed and when justice has been served." I started to hide my sinister smile.

"I have some medicine for you that you can use to help you sleep. Back in college I remember thinking I had everything wrong with me, because I had all of the symptoms of something. The medicine seemed to … well anyway, here are the pills if you need them. Take two of them with dinner and water."

Chapter 46

"THANK YOU. I appreciate the medicine and your hospitality, but if you don't mind, my time is valuable." I knew I was putting her at ease so I could demand a little more than what I was getting from her.

"Oh, no problem. I will keep going. Jesse was a very set man. He had everything he wanted exactly the way he wanted it. It was the control that broke us apart. He would never side with me when I was feeling upset about something or someone. He always said I was too angry with the little stuff in life and I would never truly live." I can see the softer side of her face start to show. The whole conversation, while she was talking, she looked into my eyes with confidence, except when she talked about herself. *Was she really sad? Was Jesse really like that? Or was there truly something missing in her life?*

"So you can say Jesse was always on the bright side of things in life?"

"Yes, minus a few things that he didn't believe in, but even then he reasoned and became polite about them. I don't think he would ever hurt someone intentionally. I was always worried about the way he adapted to the things in our relationship that changed.

When he became comfortable with certain things, he liked them to be exactly that way every time. Jesse never changed. He was always this great guy that everyone knew. I still have these dreams of us staying in on a Saturday night, watching movies and acting like little kids in love. I wake up from these dreams and look over at his side of the bed. But I never really had to look. He had a scent that carried throughout my house and especially on the sheets of my bed. When he went to work and I stayed here, it was like he never left. He loved being with me. He loved just doing nothing with me all day. When we were by ourselves, everything seemed perfect. I learned so much from him. I loved everything he did. He used to call me his little jelly bean."

I analyzed her words and believed everything she was telling me was genuine because of the way she looked when she spoke of these memories of him. She tried to pull off this tough look about her, but the softer her voice, the more truth I derived from her words.

"He would never, ever, tell me I was overweight, out of shape, or anything but beautiful. I knew I wasn't the skinniest girl he had ever been with, but I knew he loved me inside and out. He knew I had a temper. I hid that from him until later on in the relationship when we became comfortable with each other." *Did he? I can remember how all of my romantic relationships were perfect for the first few months and then I would start to see the truth come out.*

"Sorry to redirect you, but can you explain how you knew that you weren't the skinniest person he had ever been with?" I was not really sorry, but I knew she needed those words to calm the conversation.

"I mean, I don't know." Her confidence slowly became evident to even herself. "The only other person I know he had been with was some girl from Europe. He never really talked to her, but I met her on a couple of occasions. She was like a hippy or something. I don't think that girl even showered. I mean, her hair looked like a curly mess. She did have a pretty face and a tan I would kill for."

Holding back my own opinions on Abby I gave her a content grin. "So there was a little envy in some parts of this woman?"

"She was skinny, had a pretty face, and every single bit of Jesse's attention." The truth came out in a three of a kind.

I was silent because I wanted Illek to keep talking about Abby.

"Look, I thought we were talking about Jesse."

I had to switch gears to keep this interrogation moving because I started skating on thin ice as soon as I entered this apartment. *It was still good to know the depth of her jealousy.*

Chapter 47

MY BANDAGE STARTED to bleed through. "Are you keeping pressure on that? You still haven't told me where you got this from." I was starting to feel like this was definitely all an act now. *If she would have given me time I would have changed the subject.*

"Don't worry about it. This kind of thing has happened a lot recently. Listen, I'm trying to figure out how to emulate all aspects of Jesse's life. In order to do that you must tell me what he was like through your eyes."

I understood her confusion about this concept by the way she pulled her body away from mine. I didn't realize how close she was until she moved away.

"I know that may sound weird, but the closer I become to Jesse, the closer I will get to locking up this case. Only then will I be able to rest. I have to figure out everything Jesse was a part of, up to the point of his death, to be able to see it through to the resolution."

That sparked something, as she literally pushed me away with her disgusted eyes. It was like she was a fuel piston flooded with gasoline, just waiting for a spark plug to ignite. Here comes the bitch we all know and love.

"Yeah, that's really weird. You are starting to freak me out. May

I ask why you are wearing a shirt and tie then?" After her response I began to get defensive, but she saved herself by answering my question. She wanted to help me, like when my arm was bleeding. This woman could love.

"Well, I have to investigate this very serious situation, so I must look like a professional. Is that not a good reason?"

She turned her stool, faced me and put her hands on my knees. "Exactly my point. He never dressed professionally. Not even to sorority formals. Can you believe, one time he dressed in a regular T-shirt with jeans to attend semi-formal?" She laughed and looked to the side.

"I don't really understand what you mean."

Laughing. she said, "Aha! You must be the fraternity guy who makes fun of his own fraternity by acting dumbfounded to Greek life terminology." *She was right.*

"What do you mean? And how could you decipher that from me?" I wasn't exactly concerned with what she thought of me. I was just trying to find her reason for that accusation. Also, she could have some investigative tips for me.

"He thought semi-formal meant you only had to wear semi-formal clothing. Can you believe it?" She finished her question and started to say something else. I acted like I still didn't understand.

"Semi-formal means you still dress in … well, what you're wearing. It is kind of funny now, thinking about it. I was so mad."

I nodded to say I understood and wanted her to continue with her story.

"During this time of the year, he would only wear basketball clothes, no matter where he was going to go. It used to make me so angry that he would wear these kinds of clothes to nice restaurants and bars on dates with me. I mean it would take me an hour to get ready with straightening my hair and finding the right dress that didn't make me look fat, and it would only take him ten minutes to take a shower and put on some gym shorts and a band T-shirt."

I could tell that this was one of those small things that she dwelled on. "Looking back, I have learned that I have been a bitch before I was polite. This was probably why his parents hated me." That caught my attention more than anything.

"Please explain."

"Well, I'll tell you about a situation that happened; I think this was the downfall of his parents and me. I was having fun with some of my sorority friends, drinking on July Fourth. I mean who doesn't drink all day on July Fourth?"

I was done answering questions I already knew answers to, and she was done with even allowing enough time for me to answer.

"I was supposed to come over for dinner with his parents, and I was warned by Jesse to be on my best behavior because my first impression was all I would be given with his parents. I don't know why he cared what his parents thought, because he told me so many stories about how they never showed up to anything Jesse found important. Anyway, he said that they already liked me because I was a nurse and I would be making good money, but even so, this first impression was very important. He told me his parents were strict and very traditional. I believed him, but I took it too lightly, because when he discovered I had been drinking he got very upset with me. When I got out of the car he shielded me from his parents. He sat me down and asked me how much I had to drink, and I said a few. Then he asked me what the difference was between me and an alcoholic."

I was trying to hold back my laughter because of how it made her feel to hear him say that. Dark comedy has become the only amusement I can enjoy. When I saw the way it affected her, I saw her missing him. She needed him, but he never needed any of us.

"Well, I got upset and he told me to go home so I would not embarrass myself, but with Jesse's heart he couldn't let me drive home, because driving drunk was a very bad idea. He used to tell me that all of the time. Driving under the influence of emotions is the same as driving under the influence of alcohol. Driving with both would be twice as deadly. He was always really smart about those kinds of things. He was always so careful. That's why I don't under …" Her face dropped again. When she looked up at me, as tears rolled off her face, I looked into her eyes. Her eyes became a perfect mural with the green and blue glowing to a shine. She was beautiful when she was powerless. Her beauty came to me as soon as I dropped my preconceptions and she dropped the armor she carried to sleep with her.

I slid my stool closer to hers. I wanted to comfort her tightly, the way I wished someone would comfort me. I shared tears with her. I could not help it. We missed him. I wiped her tears from her eyes and stared at her figure. Then I gradually pulled myself away from her, still lightly gripping her arms. I asked her to keep going with her story.

"I don't understand why this happened. He was careful. He was always the person who drank the least, just in case someone needed a ride home for being drunk. Everyone trusted him."

"I know."

Chapter 48

"So that's it? That's why his parents hated you?" I was still bewildered about why his parents hated her when they never even spoke to her.

"No, I'm sorry. I got sidetracked thinking about all of the great times I had with him."

"It's okay. Please carry on because they are on my list of suspects." I knew she would say something about those words. I felt like the timing was right for me to tell her she was also a suspect. Then I thought about how much I wanted to hear the rest of the story she was telling me.

"Suspects? You've got it wrong. He—"

Once again I had to interrupt because everyone had the wrong perspective on this investigation. Everyone had given up on the fact that this was a murder. Someone killed him. "Never mind that, just keep on with your story, please. You have been very informative."

She was already taking a slow step back away from me. Her eyes squinted in a way that showed her distrust of my motives. I was losing her.

"Well, he didn't want me to drive back home because of my condition, so we decided I should stay and to sober up at his house.

He wanted me to stay until I was fully okay with driving back home, since he didn't want me there. He decided that he wanted me to come in and have dinner to sober up. I told him this was all on him." I could tell she was exceptionally skilled at blaming somebody or something else for anything that wasn't good in her life.

She looked down. I chose to believe that she was just ashamed of what she was about to admit. I didn't want to think she was lying.

"I came inside and he was talking for me, answering his parents' questions. I know if they would've given me another chance I could have shown them I am better than that. My parents absolutely adored him. They thought that wanting to become a teacher was such a novel thing to do." *At least someone has normal parents like mine.* "Anyway, it was like all of the times when I was younger and I wanted to feel drunk and it never really happened. Beer tasted so terrible I could only sip at my drink. I never drank enough to feel intoxicated. So I kept drinking and drinking until I just decided to act drunk like all of my other friends." Illek began to chuckle in a sad way. "Except think about what I just told you, but in reverse order. The more I wanted not to feel drunk, the more drunk I felt. So, needless to say, his parents, his sisters, and his friends hated me." Illek had a problem meeting new people.

She pulled her hands up, and I remembered what my mom always told me, *"Anyone with their palms up is guilty."* I think Illek's gesture was her way of looking for someone else to blame because she could never take full responsibility for any of her actions. I ended the grief I shared with her. I no longer wanted to comfort her. Even if I had proof she killed Jesse, she would find a way to pin it on something or someone else.

"I was really trying to become better, but his parents were relentless. They would never let him come on any of my family's vacations because they didn't want us to take that next step in our relationship. I really wanted that. It's the reason we broke up so many times. He had a fear of commitment because of his parents.

So I would say that almost everything that went wrong with our once perfect relationship had something to do with his parents."

The wrath of a bitch who couldn't take the accountability for anything she had ever done. First, she accused Jesse for her coming into his parents' house drunk. Then, for him having a fear of commitment because he didn't want to get married this young. And lastly, she blamed the whole situation on his parents because they raised Jesse to have a fear of commitment. I don't doubt that his parents caused a lot of what happened, but I know when something is my fault. She thought she was of some kind of higher society, one where everyone was perfect and no one made any mistakes. I felt sick to my stomach by how much I was holding back putting her in her place.

Chapter 49

EVEN WITH MY hate for her building, I had to keep this conversation rolling. "I'm sorry to hear that. I can tell he used to make you smile a lot."

"He was something I wasn't used to. He wasn't in an everlasting love with me. It was because he did not fall in love with me when we slept together, that I loved him. In fact, he wouldn't even sleep with me the first night he stayed over at my apartment. We kissed, and he made no advances to take off my clothes. Even though I wanted him to touch me, Jesse just passively cuddled with me. The desire we built up for each other flourished that night."

"Was this the first time you met?" Jesse never talked about any of this with me before, so I had to pry.

"Yes. I can admit that as a freshman and sophomore in college I was a bit easy. I met him at a party one night at my friend Matt's house. Jesse was drinking a cup of water in a corner of the room. His hair was all shaggy and his jeans were tight. At first, I thought he was one of those guys who, because of his red Solo cup, pretended to drink a lot and take advantage of girls who partied too hard. Something about him turned me on. His shy presence could have been misconstrued for insecurity, but when I talked to him that all changed. I sat down next to him, and we talked for a while. He spoke about doing something with kids and how he loved to see them grow. I drank more and more. It wasn't until my seventh drink that I found out he was drinking water. I felt stupid for drinking so much, but I still wanted him to come home with me. He was reluctant at first, which made me want him more. He drove me home after dropping off three other friends. I invited him inside my apartment and inside of me. He chose to make sure I was okay and told me that he had too much respect for me to take advantage of my inebriated state. The next morning he kissed me and left. I thought for sure he would give in to my desires when he saw me half naked next to him. If he hadn't kissed me, I would have never thought he liked me. He was someone I had to work hard for, to earn his love. And to be honest with you, I don't exactly know how he fell in love with me. Or if he even did."

I hated when people started by saying, "well, to be honest with you." *What the hell do you mean?* Have you been lying this whole time, and now, finally, you want to start telling the truth? I could tell my mood was shifting more and more, even though the story affected certain parts of my body that could not be controlled.

"Eventually we did go on dates, and we started our three-year journey from there. When I really got to know him, I found that he was not insecure or shy. I think Jesse just looked for the right words to say. He was a man of few words around people he didn't know. He was the nicest guy I have ever met. Without even sleeping with me, he did anything I wanted him to do. My favorite part about him was that he did not care about what others told him about me. He loved me no matter what person I used to be. It was so normal for me to have someone who would give me everything I wanted right from the start, with no effort on my part. I never had to work for that kind of stuff. Once I got Jesse, I had him wrapped around my finger. He even said that he could see us going the mile together. But he still never changed for me. He never sat with me to make fun of the people passing by, like my sorority sisters and I did. He never drank during the day with me either. He always saw the best in all of the people I judged. He apologized every time for the things I would say, even if they were things I wouldn't take back. He never changed his happiness."

"Did you want him to not be happy?"

"No. I just wanted him to side with me. He never sided with me."

"I'm sorry; so what do you mean when you say you had him wrapped around your finger?"

The truth started to pour out uncontrollably when she placed her hands down on the counter. She had been talking with her hands the whole conversation until she said this, "I mean he wasn't going to leave me. He could never leave me. I could tell he was in too deep with me. I controlled our relationship, where it was going, what we were doing, and even why we dated. Whenever it came down to something that had to be done on his end, he did it. All I had to do was a little convincing. I had to tell him why he was with me. And if I ever had his parents' goddamn permission I would have had him as my husband. Even though he would never commit, I had him going nowhere else but with me. He loved me."

"Was Jesse always happy about things with your relationship?"

"Yes, he had to be. He was always looking for the bright side of anyone or anything. If you want to be more like Jesse, then be happy all of the time. Laugh at everything, because if you can't, you shouldn't be doing it. He constantly told me that quote, over and over."

Laugh at everything you do, because if you can't, you shouldn't be doing it. That was something I could use in my investigation.

Chapter 50

"SPEAKING OF QUOTES …" She finally started to reveal her secrets about him. "He basically lived his life off of the stupid quote he got from a blind man. Jesse used to work at the neighborhood pool where he grew up. Well, mostly he volunteered as a lifeguard and swimming coach. He used to help a blind man named Arthur get to the swimming lanes, and Jesse showed him how many steps his chair was away from the lanes. He talked about him all of the time. Arthur was the happiest man he had ever met. He said Arthur used to have this permanent smile that felt contagious to Jesse. I could tell whenever he saw Arthur because he would be even happier about the world than he was before. Arthur told him the same thing every time Jesse asked him how he was doing. "How's it going with that girlfriend of yours?" "Oh, it's going just fine. Thanks for asking. How are you doing?" Jesse told me what Arthur said. Arthur had the same response each and every day. He said, "It's always a good day when I wake up breathing and nobody's shooting at me." He let quotes like this run his life. He enjoyed seeing the way other people lived."

Jesse was easily inspired. He had to be easily inspired because he always told me one thing about teaching too, "As a teacher, you don't

189

teach kids, you inspire them."

"Arthur had a big impact on his life and his outlook on how the things in the world were great and nothing was as bad as it seems. Arthur eventually stopped coming to the pool, and Jesse only had his ideologies to remember him." I still did not understand why Illek was so angry. *What angered her? How did Jesse's life not influence Illek like it did for me?*

I saw why Jesse and Illek had so many problems. The way little things went by Jesse like nothing and Illek liked to stay in one spot over a situation. But if Jesse was so good at letting the little things go and moving on, *why couldn't he leave Illek for good?* It seemed as if he stayed around with her for some reason and I haven't grasped that concept as of yet. "Why did he stay with you?" I feared her response. "If he didn't like the way you handled things and the way you carried yourself?" I knew that this answer, if she would answer it, would be a defensive proclamation.

"Jesse was really fond of watching and making people grow in life. The night we first met, after I was already three sheets to the wind, he told me I was a puzzle that hadn't been put back together yet. And I know you're probably thinking that's something you didn't want to hear as a girl."

My face showed her she was correct.

"But then he said, 'I'll fill in your missing pieces, and we'll make a masterpiece.' I wanted to be better, and he was helping me more then he knew, but I never let him know. That's why he wanted to become a teacher. He loved watching the kids grow. Helping kids improve on anything is what gave him the aspiration to become a teacher, even when he knew the government was getting rid of educators and budget cuts would give new teachers no chance of getting a job. But those people, who didn't hire him, really damaged his self-esteem. I could tell he was getting so anxious and his hopes were fading. He always had something to say that helped me believe he was all right. I couldn't be Jesse. I couldn't tell him the positive

things he always told me when I was down. He never stopped looking at the bright side. Not ever, even when his dad never came
home. Even when his mother doubted his career choice, he smiled.
He smiled when both of his parents ..."

I had to interrupt before she said anything else about that, "I
know about his parents. I will be meeting with his mother soon. I
will make sure I get her perspective on Jesse's life. Thank you for
yours."

I wanted to know what other people thought of Jesse. I did not
want the perception of one suspect to color the image of another
suspect. It would be too easy for a guilty suspect to redirect the
responsibility. I was very focused on the idea of keeping a grip on
this case.

Chapter 51

I DON'T THINK she heard me as she started to cry again. *How could she have any bodily fluids left?* She became an extension of my shoulder.

"Jesse, I don't want to be who I was back then, I never wanted to lose you. I could lose any one of my friends and everything I owned to keep you here with me. Why?"

Considering she hated new people, this wasn't normal for her. When she let her guard down, being compassionate and affectionate was easy to do. But she insisted on hiding compassion and truths behind her stone wall skin. She felt secure keeping those feelings inside of her.

"He helped me through so much. Now that he's gone I've thought about my time with him. I want to remember all of the good and forget the bad. I know I'm a better person because of him. I'd slit my throat to bring him back."

Would she? I pondered that statement for a bit.

"I miss him so much."

She had her hands cupping her small face. I stood up from the stool and placed my hand on her shoulder because I knew she would know what I was about to say next. "Well, I have really got some great stuff here, Illek. Thank you very much for being a great suspect."

At that moment I saw the transformation of her emotions. I pictured her in a blanket of pain. I wanted to hear her squeal and yell when I completed her request. I wanted her to have her last memory of life being scared, helpless, and powerless. Like every good movie, the antagonist changes from the first scene to the fade-out. She came into this world as a puppet master, and I wanted her to leave as a puppet. I was outside myself.

"What?" She exposed her face and her personality as she twisted her palms up. She stopped sobbing. "What did you say?"

I could see it coming. Anger and fear together. The timing was not yet right. I couldn't wait to hear her scream. I remembered that terrible night. The night where she slammed the door and left him there; left us there. I remember that he didn't use his call for her. He used it for his parents. Then he used it for me. *It's not over yet. There is still more to uncover.*

"Good day."

When I walked toward the door to leave, it slightly stabbed my leg, and I endured the pain silently. My mom gave me this knife for Christmas. It came in a set with a knife sharpener. It was a gift intended for my new apartment for my new roommate and me to use. She was speaking, but I could not hear her. I loved pain. It was a physical reminder that I was alive. There were times when I felt like I was only dreaming.

I left smiling and thinking about her last request. "She would cut her throat to bring him back." She was starting to become fatalistic, and I loved it. I smiled and walked away.

Chapter 52

THE SCARIEST THING in the world to see is the light indicating your life has ended as you know it. Our light was not like the light they talked about in movies or books. They spoke of a white light that swallowed you whole, like you were in a room with white walls, floors, and ceiling. Our light was white, blue, yellow, and red. We could not escape this light without consequences.

I looked over at Jesse. Sweat and tears was what I expected, but he was calm. He sat there with both hands on the steering wheel. He stared forward because he knew that if he looked at me, the reality of what just happened would be too much to bear. He had to be calm. He had to accept this life-altering mistake we just made because there was no other choice. He knew this was going to end his life and he could do nothing.

Meanwhile I planned all of the ways I could get out of this car. I was going to run. I had to run, and I knew Jesse wouldn't come with me. The innate instinct of survival took over as my hand wrapped around the door handle.

"Jesse man, I got to go."

He just stayed there in his seat, frozen. Emotionless and selfless, he sat in my seat facing forward. I couldn't wait any longer, especially since it became even more of a reality when the flashlight hit the reflection of the side mirror into my eyes. I knew we were dead. *They* did not like rich college kids in this neighborhood.

I felt the selfishness of my decision grow when the un-clicking of my seatbelt echoed through the car. I took one last look at Jesse before I opened the door. He stared out of the windshield, probably thinking about how close we were to being home. He never moved, and I didn't know what to do, except escape. My conscience went back and forth about whether or not I should run. The decision was made.

The devil in me won. I jumped out of the car. I jolted into a sprint and ran faster than I have ever run before. It felt like they were right on me. I knew a shortcut that would bring me back to Poe Street from Walker. Through these woods I escaped my death. I couldn't hear them anymore, and I stopped.

The thin branches that hit me as I ran by reminded me that I left my best friend to die. I left him to die alone. My mind stopped about thirty seconds before I got into the woods, when they told me to stop, "Hey come back here you son of a bitch." My mind told me to stop and help Jesse. My body kept running through the woods to protect myself.

I ran a little further until I reached the end of Poe Street. I could still hear their voices like the shrill of sirens to my eardrums. I knew *they* never saw my face so I was safe as long as I got back onto the campus. I fell to my knees crying. My friend is dead now. His life is over. I knew I was safe, but the cost of my safety was his life. I knew what I had to do now.

I thought about calling someone or running to someone else's house to get help. I had to gather myself before I ventured out. *I have to help him myself.*

Chapter 53

IT SEEMED LIKE a piece of Jesse was in every one of the suspects, like every one of the suspects lived their life through Jesse's life. No matter how I looked at it, he was a very well-liked person by many people. People saw him as the role model kid. A kid that they all wished they could go back and be. He had everything and lost it all. I was put here to change that. *No, I put myself here to change that. Nobody had a plan for me. I made my own goddamn plans.*

I was driving back to my apartment complex when I noticed my body; I had not slept in days. I could not sleep because even when I closed my eyes, I saw him. His face was condemned to an image forever. My dilapidated memories of him started to break me down, so I chose not to rest. Sleep was for the weak.

It was almost like his face had an emotion of surprise like he didn't see it coming. But when they came for him, he knew what he was about to go through. Jesse knew that they put him there for the sole purpose of him dying that night. I really should carry a gun in there and shoot every one of the guys. There were too many of them for me to kill and live. His parents and the other suspects were more responsible for letting them do this. They had to be responsible.

I loved when I was around Jesse. I felt better about myself. It was almost like we took pieces away from Jesse to the betterment of ourselves and the diminishing of him. He taught us so much about being an important person of society. He allowed people to give him advice, but unlike the rest of us, he actually took the advice and lived the way people told him would bring him satisfaction. I would have to admit that if Jesse had any flaws, it was that he always listened to people he trusted. Even though his parents were not people he necessarily trusted to guide him, he still obeyed and appreciated their words. He was just searching for himself in all of these people. And all of these people were searching for themselves in him.

Where did fatalism come into his life? I had to get to the bottom of this. Someone changed him from the happiest most positive philanthropist to a dark horse.

I passed my parking deck on campus and kept driving because there was something about this drive that calmed me. I had interrogated five suspects and found four of the six responsible.

On campus people looked so happy. *Why were they so happy? What was making them smile and feel happy?*

There was nothing in life that was as good as people wanted you to believe. There's only a built-up expectation that falls in the sight of realism, but we're so happy about it that we settle for what we receive. That is what it's like for everything in this world. Sex was not as good as people tell you it was. It was only the accomplishment of conquering another person's secret. You are allowed to touch areas on a person that had only been seen by a few. You have a boat of confidence that floats high in the sailing winds because you were allowed to enter that person's body. But it was not like they said it would be. They said it was an instant pleasure. Something that would be the greatest feeling you'd ever feel. It's not. The only thing that made sex desirable was the idea of being inside of someone else's body. There was no great feeling of instant pleasure, only the gratification conquest. When it was too easy, it was not enjoyable, and when it was too hard, we'd give up. Nothing was ever as good as it seemed …

I had to have a journal because Jesse had one. I understood why he had one now. A journal was a way of remembering. Clearly, it was a way to express what went wrong and what went right. I decided to write journals on all of my suspects and explain why they were responsible for his death. It was going to have many conflicts and a big ending. My eyes started to dilate with the excitement at the thought of how this story would end. *I couldn't wait.*

I started writing down notes of the questionings so far. "In my visit with Georgio, it was never as good as it seemed with numbers, but numbers spoke the truth. Jesse understood numbers and truth through Georgio. Jesse became depressed when it took him longer than he expected to find a job. He became even more depressed when his father figure pressured him into a career he did not want to pursue. Not because he absolutely didn't want to be a pool man, but because he thought of the pain it would cause to refuse an offer from Georgio. He wanted to make Georgio happy, and this is one of the reasons this suspect could be held responsible for his death. Jesse wanted to make him happy, and he couldn't do it because he already had his own dreams. This was where he became conflicted with two ideas of what he wanted to be and only one true way to happiness. He felt like his dreams were too selfish and at the same time he couldn't please Georgio. Jesse had the pressure built up inside of him. I guess that was why he never called her back. His dreams of becoming a teacher were destroyed by the only woman he looked up to as a role model. Bea was his mother. Bea was his mother, and his mother was his mother. It made sense. All this time I knew I should've convicted her. Bea destroyed his dreams. Georgio's dreams destroyed him, and his only love ran away twice because of a witch."

I started a new page section titled, "Questions I Still Didn't Have Answers for Yet. Why did he not call her back? Why would he have his dream right there in front of him and not call back? I know he listened to that message before he was taken that night. I knew because the message was skipped on his voice mail. Was he leaving me a clue to his murder? The reason I asked these questions was because if he had totally given up on his dreams why would he only skip the message? Why wouldn't he just delete the message? There was something I was missing."

"First skipped message sent Friday, September 9th at 1:00 p.m. eastern time. Jesse, this is Danielle Fullwood at Joyner Jones Elementary with Onslow County Schools. You interviewed with us a couple of weeks ago. I just wanted to say personally I was very impressed with your interview, and we have some exciting news for you. Please give us a call back at (912) 207-8904. Thank you and we look forward to speaking to you again."

I started another page section titled "Possible Answers to Questions That Have Been Raped by Evidence in All Kinds of Manipulative Ways. Abby told him that she loved him and he was going to live with her across seas? No, that is too farfetched. There would have been some kind of evidence like packed bags or a website history that had apartment complex prices in Spain or something. That couldn't be true."

I knew that the pool business was proposed to him by Georgio and that caused an overwhelming weight upon Jesse's back. "Maybe Georgio pressured Jesse. Maybe he knew Jesse was folding his dream and he pressured him until he gave in. He was his father-figure; Jesse had to listen to him because he trusted him." *No, that can't be it. Georgio was only offering a backup plan for Jesse, and I couldn't do anything but trust him. He wouldn't want this to happen to him. I could tell when I saw him at the funeral. He was the most broken one in the whole crowd. He couldn't have done it.*

"Abby moved away like the wind. She was his lover. Nothing and no one compared to her. He told me this, in his journals. She wouldn't have killed him, I know it. She would only want the best for him, just like Georgio. She couldn't have done it. Maybe she'd planned a way to get rid of Illek." The thought of that seemed irrationally calming to my nerves.

It was like a pencil with an eraser at both ends. I started to rip up the papers I had written before. I was losing hope in finding the responsible when I remembered that the only scenario that made sense was Illek. That manipulating, controlling bitch, she did it! She manipulated my thoughts with her false concern for my health. My teeth cracked as I clinched the knife once again. I had to feel what Jesse felt, and she had to feel what it was like to be responsible. "She controlled Jesse. Onslow County was four hours away from where Illek worked. That bitch." I have never wanted to kill someone as bad as I do now. I became obscene. "She told him that he couldn't accept the job because it was too far away. She gave him the ultimatum that all controlling women use with men. If you do this, then this is what will happen. With someone like Jesse, there was no real choice for him. He only wanted to make her happy and that's what he was going to do at any *expense.* She told him that if he decided to take that job he was going to lose her. I had to kill her now."

I peered around, looking for anything I could use to persuade her to confess. All I saw was the large book that I turned my back on. *But nothing was going to stop me now. Even if He stepped down in front of her door, He, Himself couldn't stop me.* If He did come down right here, right now, I'd tell him to "Bring it." She was already dead, and my knife would work. If we were all just a structure where our own savior sits, then I'm a little black house, and no one's living in it. I turned the book upside down, feeling faithless and exhausted. I was Jesse's bloody arms.

I ran down the stairs from my fourth floor room. I skipped steps and heard my ankles popping out and back into place. I couldn't feel anything. All I could do was think about how she was going to look when an emotion condemned her face. She'd have an emotion not only of shock, but dismay that she had no control. She would have that expression on her face forever. No matter how many pounds of embalming fluid they injected inside of her. She would always have no control over any more of her manipulating expressions. I was laughing inside. It felt right. I knew it was right. She needed to pay the price for leading him to his death. They killed Jesse because Illek kept him here when his life was taking him elsewhere. She condemned him.

I was running down the street like Jesse did. Jesse wrote about a time when Illek got hit by a car walking to class one day. When Jesse got the call from the emergency team, he ran like I was running. He cared so much about her, and she wasn't deserving of one single fiber of his body. He said he was taking a test for a health class. He got the call and ran out of his exam, pencil and paper still lying on the foldout desk. He ran to the hospital from campus, six miles away.

I had the same sense of urgency. I had to do what I needed to do before I thought about it too much and talked myself out of it. I got into my car, and it seemed like every stoplight was working in my favor. I didn't worry about road rage because no one got in my way. I had all of the anger I could take before my ears burned off the sides of my face and my nails went through the palm of my hands.

I drove to her apartment. I banged on the door and realized that if I was going to get inside of the building she would only let me in with the assurance that it was okay. I knocked gently again and again. She was probably still crying so hard that she could not hear me knocking. I took her silence as permission to come in because she wanted me to, so I walked around back. I looked up at her room and couldn't see any lights or movement. I couldn't leave without knowing if she was or wasn't there.

I looked around for rocks to throw at the window. I couldn't find anything so I took the liberty of breaking the window next to the back doorknob and unlocked the deadbolt. I walked on the broken glass on the floor. It still smelled like it did when I came here the first time. It smelled like a clothing store mixed with a hospital. I couldn't find any trace of her, but in case one of her roommates popped out of somewhere, I had my knife tucked away. I would never want to have to kill someone out of fear that they may be speaking to the people who killed Jesse. I walked upstairs, forgetting that she had no more roommates. She ran them all out with her controlling personality and inability to be happy.

I opened the door and took a deep breath because I knew I would forget to breathe when I started having fun going inside of her. I loved the smell of flesh. I especially loved the smell of freshly carved flesh. I craved it now like a dog after his first taste of human blood. All I have smelled was my own, and I couldn't wait to smell the flesh of one of the responsible. As my eyes adjusted to the dark I saw she wasn't there. The room was empty. *Did she go out the front door when I broke in? Did she hear me throwing rocks at her window and try to hide?* I searched and searched for her in all of the places she could have been. I ripped that place apart like a madman on cocaine dancing with classical music in his head. Kicking and swinging the knife, cutting the air open. I flipped over the mattress and knocked down the doors and started to grin. *I had to find her now.* It was almost like a game to me. I became crazed with the obsession of seeing her again.

She wasn't there, and I wasn't exactly angry, I was excited, like when you have an overwhelming need for a girl to sleep with. I hated sluts. They were so easy I could barely get a nut off. I loved a challenge that would take work to receive the payoff. I think I was wrong when I said nothing is as good as it seems. I couldn't imagine feeling that good about killing someone.

I drove to her work. She had to be there. I knew it was going to be a public place, but I didn't care anymore. I knew what my own fate was telling me to do. Make the responsible feel the pain of loss; the pain of truth. The truth in numbers couldn't match with the truth of a knife.

I went into the hospital and remembered something Jesse told me one day. *He told me about the first time he met Illek's parents, ironically, in a hospital. She was hit by that car and he ran to the hospital. He said he almost beat the ambulance to the hospital. He stayed with her until she woke up. He told me she knew Jesse loved her when he kissed her. I mean, you would have to love someone to kiss a face like that. She had road rash on her lips and cheeks, two black eyes, and a broken nose. Her parents were so thankful that for the two months that they had been together. She finally found someone who cared about her.*

They told him all of these crazy stories about the ex-boyfriends. Her most recent breakup was with some guy named Chris Hyatt. Hyatt used to beat her and slash her tires and do all sorts of crazy things. They talked about one night when he came to their house and put a gun to Illek's head and said, "It will be you who feels no more last words." I was easily convinced that she made him crazy. Her controlling, manipulating personality drove people insane.

Jesse's stories about her parents were so positive. He loved them from the moment he met them. It must have been when they told him he was welcome into their home anytime. I wonder if her parents were the only reason he stayed with her so long.

I had calmed down from my earlier rampage. I came into her apartment and destroyed everything, and it was a real horror show to see what she would look like dead. I couldn't wait for the expression on her face. I brought in the wind from outside.

I danced my way to the reception desk. The lady was getting upset with one of the patients waiting to be seen by a doctor. "Sit down, sir. The doctor will call your name momentarily. You need to sit down." I knew she was already upset and it was going to be hard to have her let me inside to see Illek.

"Yes sir." I forgot I was standing there staring at her. I looked down at her name tag to address her with respect. I knew that was how I was going to be allowed in there.

"Hello Amanda, I have a request." I spoke with clear confidence, and I hadn't looked to see what I looked like anymore, but I think it was working. She smiled.

"Most people don't even take the time to look at my name tag. What can I help you with?" It worked.

"Oh, I think it is one of the simplest ways of being polite." I really didn't give a shit about being polite, but I gave one of those old-time smiles. Being polite was just another way of hiding the truth, so I carried on, "I have an urgent message I need to give a nurse in the Intensive Care Unit."

"Well, I'm not supposed to send anyone but medical personnel to that unit for any reason, but how about I call her down here to meet with you?" My eyes lit up.

"You would do that for me? You're sweet and very kind. Thank you." I placed my hand on the desk, bringing our proximity closer.

She laughed and was about to ask what her name was when the idiot patient from before walked back to interrupt our conversation.

"I see how this works. You're in here getting dates and stuff ... and you can't help people like me."

"Sir, I am not going to ask again. You will be seated, or you will get your doctor's visit wearing handcuffs around your wrists. You choose, sir."

"Lady, I have chemicals in my eye. I can't see anything in front of me."

She picked up the phone and called down to security. I turned around to face him. "What the hell is your problem, man? Everyone is trying to get help here. Emergencies first."

"Oh shit. I don't feel half as bad as you look." He walked away from me and looked back frequently to see if I followed. I asked myself that same question. *What did I look like?* He kept looking back as he went back to his seat. He was almost scared of me. *What have I become?*

"Thank you and sorry about that. What was the nurse's name again, sweetheart?" *Why wasn't she scared of me?*

"Her name is Illek Ericson."

"Okay, just have a seat right there in the waiting area, and I will bring her right down." She pointed toward the room that I didn't want to go into. I would rather die than have to listen to the moans of those sick people.

"Yes ma'am, just tell her it's urgent and she shouldn't be worried because everything is falling into place."

"And who shall I say is here for her?"

"Jesse."

Chapter 54

I WALKED INTO the valley of the shadow of death. I was in a room closed in with people accompanied by misery and agony. I felt like I could make them all happy with a simple slit to the throat and put an end to all of the groans. I didn't understand why there weren't background noises from before that caught my attention like this place did. The sound of the agony and the smell of old sick flesh started to make me nauseous. I didn't like this smell of flesh. The mixture of their misery and hospital cologne was sickening.

I had to stay here and wait for her to come down. After our last conversation, I didn't know if she would meet me here in the lobby. I would have to surprise her or show some kind of false remorse for how we ended our conversation. I just needed her to tell me she was the reason he didn't take the teaching job in Onslow County. If she confessed, that was all I needed to take care of her.

For what felt like an hour, I sat in my seat trying to plan a scheme to get up to the Intensive Care Unit. While I was thinking about getting a doctor's scrubs and walking straight through the door, *I remembered Jesse writing something about him feeling like he was a monkey in a man suit when he was out with Illek and her friends. He was always alone, even with her right beside him. It was like Jesse was a tool in her tool kit. She just put him on the belt when she didn't need him; he couldn't get far away. When she needed him, he was right there waiting patiently to obey the wishes of her command.*

"Hey, what's wrong with you? What are you doing here?" I was surprised she even came down. I thought she would be afraid. *She would be if she saw her apartment right now.*

"Oh. I just wanted to talk." I was testing the waters on whether she was going to let me talk with her or not.

"I can't right now. I'm a little busy. Are you all right? What's going on?"

"Well, I wanted to ask you something and then apologize for the way I acted when I left your apartment." Lying through my teeth, I had to break some of Jesse's morals to get to the bottom of this. *Whatever morals I needed to give up. Whatever it takes.*

"Okay. Let's go back to my mother's office, and we'll talk a little." She took my hand, and I started to feel the butterflies in my stomach as the blood rushed to my face. I was ready to kill her and end this investigation. She was the reason Jesse died. She brought those dark hands of life to strangle Jesse. I was ready to end her.

"Mandy, call Jason at the ICU desk and tell him I am on my lunch break." I became extremely excited thinking of what was about to happen. I wanted to leave a face for them to remember, a face like Jesse's. So I gave a sinful wink to the medical coder, and we went upstairs.

The hallways were jam-packed with people, all with agendas. Everyone had a place to be and someone to tend to. We went inside her mother's office, and she closed the door. I didn't know exactly where to start because I wanted to get straight to the point, but I needed to hear her say it. I knew if she became angry with me she wouldn't say it.

"What's going on?"

"Illek, I have a question, and I desperately need you to tell me the truth." Little did she know, she could avoid being killed by simply denying that she had held him back, but I was determined to get it out of her somehow.

"Listen." She placed her hands together, wanting to speed this visit up. "Whatever you want to know I will tell you. Trust me. I know this has been hard for you. We have a psychologist for people who works on these kinds of things. He is on this floor. So if you wanted to … No one should see what you had to witness, Danny. I will help you."

I was starting to break down when my eyelids became dams cracking because the tears that filled the dam were overflowing. I had to be strong and do what needed to be done. "Illek, I heard a message from a principal from Onslow County Schools." She didn't respond, and I started to think that she was about to tell me a lie, so I paid close attention to her face. "They were going to offer Jesse a job." Her head started to tilt downward like a screw was loose in her neck and the weight of her head was unbearable to hold.

She started crying on my shoulder, and I sat down with her in my lap. "Oh … my God. He loved the beach. That would have been a dream job for him."

She didn't know. I had to make sure she wasn't bluffing. I picked her head up, ready to break her neck if she said it. "Did you know about this?"

She was sobbingly saying, "No. It must have been after he …"

"No, it was before that night. You knew about this, right?" I shook her head and almost forgot my own strength, like the man I read about in *Of Mice of Men.* I was hurting her.

"Stop. Stop. Stop." I stopped, and I thought as soon as I let go of her she would run away, so I kept my hands close.

"Did he not get the message?"

"I hope you're telling the truth because I am so close to the end of this investigation, I can feel Jesse inside of me. He got the message. It said it was a skipped message so he got it. He didn't save it or delete it. And I know that if he was going to be offered something like this he would've gone. So tell me why didn't he go?"

"I don't know. He never said anything about it."

"But he knew that if he went away for a job, you wouldn't approve?"

"No, he never even mentioned that he was looking at teaching anywhere besides here."

"Don't lie to me! Tell me the damn truth and let us both move on."

"You don't understand. I'm telling you the truth. He never said anything about looking for a job outside of Greensboro, much less a job offer from somewhere else other than here." She was telling the truth, and I couldn't stand it. I was so close to nothing. I had nothing. Nothing to work with. Nothing to gain. Nothing to lose except time. This investigation failed. There will be no justice for his murder. *Maybe they were right?*

I had to think of something quick because I started to feel the rush of disappointment on my shoulders. "Then you know it's your fault that we left!" I watched her sulks become deeper. "WE LEFT THAT NIGHT BECAUSE OF ..." I had a sudden dryness in my voice like someone was choking me. I tried again to finish my response, but it was like my vocal cords would only allow me to say "me" inside my head. It was as if everything everyone ever said about Jesse's murder screamed in my ears. Illek was talking, but I could only hear the symphony of voices in my head. It was my fault. If words had fingers, they'd point to me.

Illek looked at me like she knew everything I was going to do. She seemed fearful and I had to rid myself of my current mindset. I started a new idea. "Then it was Georgio's fault. He wanted Jesse for himself with the business. And Jesse couldn't take the idea of not making him proud. Jesse didn't leave here because he felt like he wouldn't be making him proud. He wanted to please Georgio by joining his business. The business would make them more like a

father and son." I started to discredit my idea when I realized that
he was just someone who cared about him. He only wanted the best
for Jesse. Goddamn it. Goddamn it. Goddamn it. Goddamn it.
This whole investigation had gone wrong. This was not how I
planned it.

The heftiness of the cement tightened around my feet.

Her facial expressions were nothing but the truth. I couldn't even
pretend she was lying. "I'm sorry. I just need to go home now."

The door opened. "Illek, is everything okay in here?" The doctor
looked like he used to play baseball. He had a build to him that
showed through the scrubs. The shape of his chest puffed out of the
white coat he wore. He was concerned about Illek, and that made
me think. *Is this Jesse's replacement? Has she already moved on? Why
has everyone moved on but me?*

"Yes, Dr. Starbuck, he was just leaving." She briefly stopped her
moping and wiped away her tears to show that she was all right.

"Okay, just making sure."

He left, and I was lost again. *What am I doing? Am I just a hur-
ricane filled with a forgotten past? Am I doing anything good for Jesse?
For me?*

I walked out of the room, leaving her weeping on the floor.
When I crossed the hallway of the ICU, I dodged out of the way of
a speeding patient on a hospital bed. He was asleep, and it was
probably a good thing because he was bleeding through the blanket
over his chest. I thought to myself, *I just want to sleep so I don't have
to feel.* I had used up all of the fumes I had been running on for
weeks. I hadn't mentally or physically rested in a month. I had to
go back to the room and figure out another plan.

I went down the stairs back to the lobby where I met Mandy.
When I went past her desk, I had a slow creep to my step. I felt like
the walking dead when I approached the waiting area. I felt the
wind from every breath make a slight moan as I exhaled. I tasted
the smell of dying people in my mouth. I saw a reflection through

the window of the sliding doors, and I didn't recognize the stranger I'd become. I was the walking dead.

Chapter 55

I GOT INTO my car, but this time I was disheartened. I felt again like my whole investigation was written with an eraser at both ends. Every interrogation and every one of the responsible made an honest confession and their appearance of guilt simultaneously faded. I felt like I had been running on a treadmill. Every time a suspect took me off the treadmill so I could progress, I soon discovered that I simply stepped onto another rotary machine. This time my new habit became real to me. It wasn't for Jesse this time; it was for me. I used to worry about how my car looked inside and out. Now, I could care less about staining my seats. I didn't put pressure on it either because I knew it would remind me of how Illek's confession didn't bring me any closer to the truth.

I saw something that I needed to keep my life progressing. *Whatever was left of my life?* I remember asking my mother why there was a bouquet of flowers wrapped around guard rails. I was seven years old. She told me the people who made the guard rails put flowers there every anniversary of its existence. *Even at seven years old I knew she was lying.* I was heartbroken when I found out the truth. I felt like I just drove past death himself.

When I veered closer, I pulled over to read the scripture on the bouquets. I wanted to know whose death I was passing when I was on the road. I wanted to know the name of the person who died on the road I was driving because I felt like I owed it to them. I owed them a visit to their real grave site. The graveyard was just a place where their body lay; it does not contain their death. Their death is where they died, and people who die on the road have a true grave-yard. Graveyards represent everyone's thought of Jesse's death. Something that was so pampered. Something that looked sincerely supported and well kept. Jesse's death was nothing sincere. Nothing about Jesse's life was pampered. No one was supporting the real truth. People, all of a sudden, wanted to care. People wanted to be there for him. They were only there for his body's burial. They weren't there for the real burial. They weren't there to see him sink. I needed them to bring a bouquet to the room where Jesse's life really ended.

This time I didn't stop to look at the bouquet. I drove over the bridge at Wendover highway, and I stared at the object that pene-trated my veins and irrigated my eyes. I couldn't believe it. *This is exactly what I needed to keep going.* I needed to see someone care about the dead like I did. I finally found something out of the ordi-nary. There was a Christmas tree. Not only was there a Christmas tree but there were presents under the tree. Someone cared enough to put presents underneath a tree for a dead person. Someone wanted to make sure that this person wasn't forgotten. Someone made me realize that I was that person. I was the person who brought the bouquet of flowers to the true graveyard. I was the person who brought presents to put under a Christmas tree to someone who would never physically receive them. I was the person who would never give up at giving the dead exactly what was deserved.

Part V

THE PAIN OF TRUTH
WE ALL ESCAPE FROM

MY INVESTIGATION AS of right then had failed to bring me any closer to the truth. I hoped something happened fast to seal this cut back up. I am bleeding evidence but lacking an authentic declaration. I needed a mend to this hole in my case.

I walked up the stairs, not nearly as happy as the last time I was coming down these stairs. When I thought I had found the answer. When I thought there was hope for my case.

I got back to the room and couldn't sleep, for I had something else to inspire my thoughts. I still had one more set of suspects, his parents; especially his mom. I looked back at my notes and recognized that each one of the responsible had something to say about his home life.

He talked about his home life a lot in his journals. Then the stories started to turn towards Abby. Abby told him something that he had taken in as a reality for life. "No matter how much you hate your mother, you can't change the fact that she is your mother. Friends are held on by double-sided tape, either one of you could let go at any time and totally forget about one another. True friends are held on by a hinge. Although you have you swings of being really close and apart, you stay together. Family is like cement. It can get

215

discolored, but can't lose its foundation. But listen, Jesse, the difference between true friends and family is that hinges will rust away with time, and although concrete will crack, it always has a foundation."

Jesse lived his life trying to make his parents proud. A seemingly impossible task became his death.

They were the last ones to get the call before the murder. I wondered if his parents felt remorse for losing Jesse. They probably were pretending to feel pain when I saw them at the funeral. *Did they had a life insurance policy that made them a bunch of money? Did they benefit from his death? Did they plan this?* I was going to be the one to bring them down.

A tear came down from my cheek and splashed against my steering wheel. *I should have been there with him that night I left him for dead, twice.*

I had to prepare myself for this cross-examination because they were now my primary suspects. I wouldn't let them manipulate my decision unless there was evidence.

I had great parents. I had parents who would do anything for me to succeed. I had parents who supported me. My parents gave me the love and guidance I needed to become independent. Jesse's parents had been too strict in my eyes, but something was missing here, and I had to find out what. *Where was the pain originating in this family?*

What I needed to do was to keep my new excitement down a notch. I had to make them feel comfortable to let me in their home. I gathered up my questions and notes and headed toward the last stop in the investigation. After them, there were no more suspects. This murder had to be their fault, because there was no one else left.

I walked back down the steps. This time I walked with eloquence of glamour, *like I had a need for being eloquent.*

Chapter 56

I FELT THE rush of blood through my veins to my head when I drove toward their house. The neighborhood was full of pinky-up yuppies. I found it fascinating that there is a continuum of social status that could have the most terrible of home lives. It was not only the Dontaes of the world who had a deprived childhood growing up. It could be the rich too. It seemed like the rich families who could care less about how their children were growing are criminals of neglect too. Neglect was something you didn't have to have a social status to show to a child. It was free. It was natural to parents who were so selfish that they forgot what was important, the children in their lives.

Throughout my investigation I knew that his parents did not give him much attention. Jesse was a silver spoon child who had a nanny who was more of a parent than his parents were. I could just tell from the surroundings as I pulled up to the house. I stopped while I was in the car. I took another deep breath. I had to contain myself before I blew the lid off the investigation.

His house was proof that they were prodigious accumulators of wealth. *Or were they?* Maybe they had all of these commodities and no true wealth. Maybe Georgio was right. His parents bought all of the things they couldn't afford to look wealthy. They succeeded in their front of containing wealth in money, but it was obvious to me that there was definitely a void in the wealth of love. When a child became angry in this kind of family, they receive monetary things that would temporarily make them forget why their parents didn't show up to their basketball game. Another token would erase the fact that they never picked him up from practice or ever offered to carpool with anyone else on the basketball team.

Maybe everything they owned was not really owned at all. Maybe their prize possession was obtained through a lease, *which made them look guiltier.* Perhaps their house was paid off after they received the life insurance check. They needed the life insurance policy on Jesse to help pay off creditors who called them every day. They planned this. I have my convictions. I just needed them to say the words, and I would take care of the future events.

No, I can't go in like that. Everyone was guilty before they pay for someone to prove they're innocent, but how they did it was not proven yet. I needed them to tell me that they ignored his call. I needed them to say it was totally their fault, that *they* took him away. *I bet they told the police this wasn't an open case to be investigated anymore.* They were the reason I couldn't get any help for this case. They were the reason I am a wreck right now. I couldn't dare to look at myself. I just used my imagination because I was too scared to find out the truth. This time the breath I took might have been too deep.

They went out to eat at the fanciest restaurants among the other rich families to show off their wealth. But none of these families had true wealth. True wealth was no debt and all ownership. You don't own your children, and you are not parents of a child if you see them less than forty-eight hours a week. *How can you justify your child as yours when you are the secondary parents?* I could tell all of this by the brand new vehicles and jumbo-sized house.

Chapter 57

I FINALLY GOT out of the car. They, I mean she, had to say it in order for to go any further. I needed her to say it. Then I would know this was right. I would know I was right. His father was not a part of, or of any importance in, this case because looking for fault in a family member had to be a reflection of their time with Jesse. He spent no time with Jesse. As far as I'd known he wasn't even his real father.

I entered their house without knocking.

"Hello Da—"

"Well hello. How are you all doing today?" I am contradicting myself on the inside. *Do I really care about how they are doing?* No. *Why was I pretending like I wanted these lies people made in our short conversations with people? Why were people scared to say exactly what they feel? Why couldn't I say exactly how I felt?* With this front I felt secure enough to hide behind the door and pretended like I never came into the house.

"We're doing okay. We are finally trying to move on with our lives. And we're cleaning out the empty room upstairs. I think we are going to make it into another office. How are you doing?" Well, it's nice to see that they both joined me in a conversation of lies.

I shrugged most of the introduction off as something stupid and normal, but then I realized what they said. They were already cleaning his room. Just moved on that quickly and forgot about it all. *What kinds of parents do it that quickly?*

"Moving on? How can you rest? How can you think you are not responsible?" I left the door open and brought in the outside air from which they had been protecting themselves. My words pushed them back on their heels. The silence proved that. "How the hell can you say you've moved on?"

"Just what exactly are you doing here? We are coping with our loss, and this isn't exactly helping." I started to grin as I found Jesse's father protecting the situation he had no control over.

This was not my turf, but I knew I had the advantage, the element of surprise. I was good at the art of suspense and bringing out the words onto the table that they thought they had disposed of forever, words that they hid away from but thought about constantly. Words that could help me find the truth of Jesse. Brutal honesty kills all, the listener and the speaker.

I think we were made to have the wrong exterior. Our interior was true, while we keep our exterior constantly covered so people see exactly what they expect us to be. It's when we turn ourselves inside out that we finally discover who we truly are. I had the gift of seeing through the exterior and bringing out the insides. So, as he kept his protective exterior, I knew his interior was fearful. To him I was Jesse's death coming to take those responsible, and he was going to lose his precious trophy wife. *It's okay, you can trust me. I'll make her my trophy too. I'm thinking she would look good high in the air where her shoes could fall off and it would take a full second to hit the ground; maybe a nice rope for a necklace? Well, what do you think, Mr. Saunders?*

I was sick now.

"What is it you want?"

I spoke fast, "Something truthful ... Something to solve this case … Something to explain the reason I am here. What brought me here? Why are you one of those on the list? Why didn't you answer the last call? You were the last one with a chance to stop this." I noticed Jesse's mother had not said a word that could be considered English; instead she was trying to make words from sobs and cries. *I knew he couldn't protect her forever.*

"What are you questioning? You know what happened. Everyone knows what happened, and the quicker you realize that it was an accident, the quicker you—"

"Don't you say it! Don't say another word. Just listen to what this recorder says and tell me why he didn't leave."

I sat down the recorder, hit play and watched them react. If they thought it wasn't real or refused to believe it, I was ready to convict them.

"First skipped message sent Friday, September 9th[DM1] at 1:00 p.m. eastern time. Jesse, this is Danielle Fullwood at Joyner Jones Elementary with Onslow County Schools. You interviewed with us a couple of weeks ago. I just wanted to say personally I was very impressed with your interview, and we have some exciting news for you. Please give us a call back at (912) 207-8904. Thank you and we look forward to speaking to you again."

Their emotions dropped to the floor, and the pride they still had was the only reason they were still standing. They felt how Illek felt, helpless. They knew that it was a skipped message. A message that Jesse heard and he didn't delete it nor save it. It was a message that was floating in a voice mailbox. Eventually it would be deleted, but none of us would forget what it said.

I didn't know what to feel. *If they didn't know about this message then it was Jesse's decision to not go there. If he decided not to go there, why would anyone else be responsible for what happened?* I needed them to confess, or else I'd be the only one responsible.

"Answer! Answer me!" I only wanted to hear the truth, except now I would take a lie. I needed the lie to keep myself alive. I needed a lie to help me feel like I was right for all of the things I had done.

"Can't you see what you are doing? Look Dan—" His father decided his protection had been threatened.

"Don't call me that! I am Jesse. I am Jesse. I am Jesse!" As I screamed, I started to feel my vocal cords bleeding as if Jesse had entered my voice and was controlling what I said. I was Jesse's vocal cords ripping out of his throat. The loudest crack in my voice did not stop the horror I brought into this house. My face was like something the devil would call a masterpiece.

"Look, I know you have been through a lot, and no one should have seen anything like that in their entire life. And I know you are trying to cope—"

"Cope! You want to see how I cope? Look at my arms. Look at my goddamn face!" Screaming, I had lost it, what they call normal human behavior. Everything normal about another human being's life was absent in mine. I started with a rampage of throwing fists into my face so they could see the blood of Jesse. I couldn't feel anything. I must have had just enough nerve endings in my body to keep my legs walking. Physical pain was something I no longer had. Emotional pain was something I would *forever* forget.

"I know this is hard." Mrs. Saunders was still screaming. "I'm sorry to see you like this, but we can't help you. We have nothing to offer."

We all calmed down. I spoke with a soft utter before I blew up again, "Nothing to offer?" I'd rather hear a lie than an answer like that. I had to leave before I folded.

"Yes, now please come back at a better time."

"Nothing to offer? Are you kidding me?" I was assertive. I came in with the wrong attitude. I knew if I was going to benefit from this meeting I was going to have to come in with another perspective. I was going to have to make them comfortable to get them to talk. It was too late for that, they were never going to let me in, but

I was still standing there, waiting for them to say something. But they weren't going to say anything to benefit me. I had overstayed my short welcome. But I had to get this pain off of my chest and into their arms. I exploded, "Nothing to offer? I bet you had nothing to offer. You couldn't offer your son exactly what he needed to have to end this before it started. You could've stopped this. This is your fault as much as it was anyone else's fault on the list. Don't you ever forget that!"

I had let my emotions into my investigation, and it was hurting me worse than the blood running down my arm. Physical pain was the only hurt I could bear when I came back to myself. When I became Jesse this pain was nothing more than the habit of life that kept me going. When I was Jesse, I couldn't feel any physical pain. At least I didn't show that I was hurt, because as I found out from all of these suspects, nobody knew pain better than him.

It was something that kept the pain as physical as possible because the pain on the inside was rubbing the skin raw. My nerves were firing, but my brain was not receiving the signals anymore. My insides were dead. There was no more compassion. All I had was this case and exactly how I wanted to even the score.

"Go! Please leave." I wanted to smile, as Mr. Saunders was crying now. What it must take for a man to feel his skin unfold and have his library of emotions falling all over the floor. He was desperately trying to find more and more of himself that had broken apart, spread out past his reach. Every time he thought he was through picking up the pieces, more of him came out as he cried profusely. His grasp wasn't big enough to carry it all. His insides were spilling out. *It was like when you have too many small things in your arms; once one of them falls out, the rest lose their foundation when you try to save the one you lost.* Mr. Saunders only had a short stack of feelings left.

He was almost as broken as I was.

"You have been great suspects. I will be back soon." I finally showed my smile when I left because this was a seed to my investigation that was going to grow into something worth watching when the end came near.

A smile with a side of tears, please.

Silence left with me as she started to taste the bitter flavor of her own tears. I left that house with proof that couldn't prove anything. But I could tell that it would come. I didn't want to give up like after I met with Illek. The day would come where I would get rid of all ties to this murder. I knew it would be easier to do that now. I knew what I had to do. I knew what must happen. It was all a matter a time now.

Chapter 58

I STORMED OUT of the house laughing. They gave me the truth, or at least a lie, that helped me keep going. *I didn't care anymore. Even if I thought it was real, then I felt justified.* I looked at the neighborhood and tried to visualize what it would look like when all of this came crashing down. Maybe I'll light a match to this place and watch it burn with them inside. I could smell their flesh crackling from the unstoppable flame, and no one would stop that from happening, like nothing stopped Jesse from dying.

I opened the door to my car and took a deep breath. I felt like I was almost going to quit this investigation like everyone told me I should have done. But I was about to prove them all wrong. She was going to confess. I just knew it. I knew she would not say anything because he was there. She was holding something back. Mr. Saunders was the only reason she was standing. She would have fallen apart if he hadn't held her up. I just had to get her to confess her guilt in his murder.

I drove back with no fear of what consequence my reckless behavior would bring me. I drove back with an objective, waiting for them to call. I figured she would come to me when she was ready. For the first time in this investigation I was predicting something. It was also the first time I ever waited for anything to happen in the case. Everything else that had happened in this investigation occurred because of my actions. Nothing happened for me. I had to get all of the information about Jesse on my own. No help from anyone. Finally, someone was going to come to me. I just knew it.

I had to stop thinking about the events before I met with the Saunders. Every time I thought about how close I was to giving up, the more I thought about what the police told me. "Son, I know how you feel right now. It isn't easy when something like this happens to your friend. You have to accept what happened and forgive Jesse for making a bad decision." *It's not his fault. It never was.* I just had to prove it to them. I already had so much information that they didn't know, but I wasn't going to tell them until I had all of the evidence consolidated. Half of my enragement belonged to *them*. *They* never believed me. I hated *them* because of how stubborn they were. None of them were willing to draw outside of the lines with my logic.

I was alone, especially in crowds of people. I looked over at a family. I stared at the four objects blocking the sun from my eyes. Just shadows of people. There were two parents, a child, and an electric toy car. The parents were standing so close to each other that I deciphered their conversation without seeing one word leave their lips. They are talking about how fast their little boy was growing. I saw the child looking back to see if his parents were still watching. They were present when their child needed them. In a moment I could tell that they were good parents, ones that would have a successful marriage and a caring upbringing for their child.

They were so proud of their family. Together, they had the same passion, making the best life for their child. I saw this beautiful picture, and I wanted tears to come to my eyes, but I could not feel anything. This was my life. This was the way I was raised. My body wanted me to continue staring at them, but my thoughts overpowered me. I had to look back. I glanced up at the rear mirror at the Saunders's house. Visualizing Jesse's life wasn't something I wanted to do in that very instant, but I couldn't stop. *How could I? For weeks I have been inside of Jesse's thoughts and his emotions; I have been inside his life.* I couldn't take it like he did though. "Everything's okay if you settle enough," wasn't good enough for me. It's so hard to keep putting on this mask in front of people. Normal people have to show their true emotions on the outside. People aren't supposed to congest their internal emotions.

I had been trying to keep all of this anger inside of me, and I felt it was starting to come out. My body wanted me to be those shadows. My mind would not stop telling me to look at Jesse's mirror. In Jesse's mirror, I saw two objects as clear as day. I saw a little boy alone with his electric car. When this little boy voiced his thoughts about how he felt alone, I saw his parents buying another electric car. Monetary gifts would never replace a parent's reflection in the eyes of a child, as he looked back to see if they were watching. When Jesse was making sure they were still watching, there was never anyone watching.

Chapter 59

I ARRIVED BACK at the apartment and started thinking about the information I was just presented. I remembered something that helped me picture why Jesse had such a restricted group of friends. His parents wouldn't let him become friends with Dontae because he was black and poor. They wouldn't let him further his relationship with his girlfriend because she was a drinker. Abby seemed like the only one that was accepted. *Or was it the other way around? Was Jesse the one that wasn't accepted by his own parents? He was never good enough.*

As I came to my desk I saw a few of messages on my voice mail:

"Danny, this is Dr. Babb. I still haven't received your write-up on 'Extremely Loud and Incredibly Close,' and you have missed six days of class now. I know I gave you a couple of days for you to work on your paper but not two weeks man. How many times can your printer break? Let's meet up so we can talk about this. God-speed."

"Next message."

"Danny … I got your message. You need to move on, Dan. I got a call from the Saunders. They said you came to visit them. If you ever want to talk, call me. I am ready to listen, and remember that I love you and I am so prou—"

"Message deleted."

"Next message."

"Danny ... please come back, I have to tell you something. There are things I wasn't able to tell you. I know Samuel wasn't so accepting of your visit, but I am ready to talk. Come back and meet me at the coffee shop near Bryan Park. There are some details you should know. I have come to terms that you deserve to know the truth. There are things that have not been put out in the open yet."

As if my investigation were flying at tree level, it finally reached the right altitude. A dark and seemingly endless smile cracked the skin of my cheek, as I now have all of the evidence to convict. I smiled so hard my dry skin split my lips open. I was a mess.

I looked at the mirror and broke the skin of my hand on the reflection in the mirror of a strange man. My beard was full now. Scratches, bruises, and cuts covered my face. There wasn't an open place on my face that looked healthy. I am no longer Danny. I am no longer Jesse. I was a being in a state of time that is merely a reflection of a reflection left by my predecessors. I was no longer alive but purely just an object with the chance to bring truth to a deadly lie *they* allowed us to believe. I became the needle in the haystack. I separated my life from the others, and it was time to show myself.

I walked down the stairs like the walk of the killer in the movies. The star of the movie ran as fast as she could while the killer was walking towards her. I walked by people I have seen a hundred times and said nothing to them. I wasn't the person they knew anymore. Their voices were silenced. In my ears I would only hear the confession of the murderer.

I could not focus on anything except for the road to the end. I was driving with music that only fit the scenery I saw. I drove through a green campus with the sun coming through the cracks of the trees. The shadow of the day was approaching with the tick of the long hand and the impression of the gas pedal.

I felt like people knew what was about to happen. The weird thing was that I did not feel afraid. I accepted acknowledgement of people knowing. I didn't care if they knew. I wanted them to know.

Chapter 60

THERE WAS A young man driving back home after giving his friend time to breathe. He thought to himself, 'I need to go back and check on him. I have given him plenty of time. I hope he is all right.' When the young man thought back to what happened, he started to clinch his teeth at what he could have done differently. All he wanted to do was show him a good time.

He questioned and pondered, 'I know they had to have hurt him. He doesn't look beaten, but they had to hurt him. They probably kicked him while he was down because he froze in a position on the steering wheel. They pulled him right out of the car and slammed him down on the ground. Since his face had no bruises or cuts, he landed right on his stomach. They smelled his breath as they beat his stomach until he puked. Was this my fault? I needed to talk to someone.'

Swerving lanes back to his apartment, the young man was scared to see his friend. It was four-thirty in the morning before he got back to the parking deck. He pulled into the lane with the ticket-holder machine and flashed his card. The card changed the red light to green, and the gate opened up.

The hot dog place had been closed for hours now, but the smell of boiling hot dogs still remained. The young man rolled up his windows as he drove up to the fourth level. There were only four other cars that he could see, parked in the parking deck at this time of night. He had never really seen the parking deck look so empty. During class hours, there was almost nowhere to park. It did not matter to the young man because he parked in the same parking spot on the fourth floor no matter how high the traffic of cars was.

He pulled into his spot and went over the curb a little in the front. He cursed out loud because that was the second time he had done that tonight. His car was very low to the ground and the bottom of the front bumper scraped every time he overshot the curb. He took a deep inhale and backed the car in reverse about eight inches. The car came down a half inch as he pulled away. He clicked the buttons to all of the windows at once and took the keys out of the ignition.

He got out of the car, down the steep set of stairs. He enjoyed the lack of noise the early morning brought. It brought a sense of calmness. Right before he crossed the street he stopped abruptly as a police car strolled by him. The war recommenced as his head continued to fuse his anger and depression.

His apartment sat at the end of the road near Poe Street. He walked up the stairs to the entrance of the room and listened to hear any noises coming from it. The Cone apartments were one of two tall buildings, and the lobby wasn't the best place to take note of sounds because everyone was noisy coming to and from class.

He walked over to the door from the stairway. He opened the door, looking down when a young woman screamed and dropped her hot pan full of spaghetti.

"I'm sorry; I didn't mean to scare you." He was concerned because now he had disappointed two people in the matter of three hours.

"It's okay. I just wasn't expecting anyone to be up this late. Or I guess I should say early." She gave out a small laugh, and the young man left her with no further comment. He left the girl there with her Cup of Noodles-stained pajamas.

He walked up the flight of stairs still thinking about how he could have changed the events of a few hours ago. He reached the fourth floor and put his ear up to the door of his room to see if he could hear noises. There was nothing. He thought he might have been able to hear a voice, a movement, anything that would raise a decibel. He heard nothing. He put the key into the door very gently, trying to not wake him if he was asleep. He tried to picture what the room would look like when he opened the door. Terrible thoughts streamed down into his head.

He turned the knob, hoping to see something normal. The door quietly opened, and he could see his bed, still messy from the night before. He turned the door open a little more to see his band posters on the wall. None of those posters would be there if he had not met his friend. His friend was the reason the young man started to change his life, and music was just a small influential step in the right direction for the young man. Because of his friend, he finally graduated this year and was going to begin his masters soon. The door crept open a little more, so he could see the computer he slaved over all year long. He pushed the door a little more to see his friend staring at the sheet of paper he was writing on, crouched over his desk. His friend seemed to be all right, and the young man's thought proved to be untrue. He thanked God for seeing the room the way he did and not the way he pictured.

The young man walked into the room and sat down on his bed. His body began to relax, and he contemplated talking to his friend, but he knew that they were both not in the right state of mind to talk right then. They had been through a lot that evening already. The young man slid into a slumber on top of the comforter that covered his twin-sized bed.

Across the room there was a writer, writing down words on a sheet of paper. He had already written two before this one. He did not even stop to think about what he was writing, he just continued to write. These words would change his life forever. These words would help him in the end. They would help those people understand what happened. He was not writing about the events that unfolded in front of him on the current night, instead he wrote about the situations that brought him there. He wrote LIFE in big capital letters at the top of the page.

The writer still sat at the desk he had been sitting in since his friend took him away from that awful place. The writer turned to look at his friend and wondered if he had helped him in any way. People in the writer's situation would be devastated. Something happened to him hours before that could never be replaced or restarted. 'That's a good word, restarted.' He turned back to his page and wrote more words down on the sheet of paper.

When he finished writing the last page of his letters, he stood up. His knees felt weak because he had been sitting down for hours hanging onto the words on his page. He placed the pieces of paper on the young man's chest.

He looked down as the young man was sleeping in his clothes he wore to the party. The young man was curled up in the fetal position on top of his blankets. The writer made sure he did not wake him. When he turned away to his bed he tripped over the crate that he broke before his friend came home. The crate could carry the weight of twenty books.

The writer went back to his desk to make a new plan. He wanted a plan that could ease the young man's guilt. He thought about how all of his friends would blame him. 'I'm going to be okay. I'm sorry I didn't speak to you before. I didn't know what to say. This time I wrote my thoughts down, so you can see what I wanted to say. You are a great friend.' The writer hung up his coat and put on a T-shirt. He shook the dangling socks off of his feet. They fell off halfway and never hit the ground. He laid back and tried to rest because tomorrow his life would change forever.

Part VI

THE CONFESSION. THE METAPHOR. THE CHOICE.

"HEY I KNOW what I have to do now. Thanks for being a great parent, Jesse needed that. I have found the second person. Unfortunately you know what this means. Until then, I will let my self-created fate take me."

She was crying. I knew that she could not be proud of this. She knew this call was going to end soon, and she gasped for air from her suffocating sulk. "You can't go around and do this to them. There's nothing …"

"There's everything to be done, Mom! I have to finish this. He wasn't supposed to end like this." She cared so much. My emotions were coming back up. *Push them back. Finish this, Dan. Don't let it take over. You know what has to be done!*

"Danny … STOP!" She screamed until her lungs couldn't support the output of air anymore. She knew my wind was relentless. She knew it was over.

"Good-bye."

Danny was broken. I was alive.

Chapter 61

"WELL, LET'S GO to a coffee shop. Let's go somewhere public where I can feel safe." I laughed. "Are you scared of me yet? I'll make sure that there is no stopping me from doing what needs to be done. Everyone let him down. It's time to bring them all to the table. It's time to put them in their place one by one, and I'm going to start with you because before he called me, he called you. He called you, and you did nothing. If only you knew that the next time he would call you he was only saying good-bye, and you wouldn't be able to hear it come out of his mouth before he was taken."

I paused and recognized myself looking at the foreign face again. It was the perfect person with whom to talk. It did not speak any words, instead it used echoes. It just listened and fell without trying to protect itself. It never lost its dignity. I hit it so hard and not once did it try to stop me. I felt my bones cracking. After torturing it, I continued hitting it and anything else with a reflective glare. I had no feelings anymore. My car was swerving.

I was by myself, but I really only enjoyed talking when I was my own audience. "Not as much as the professor did, but I definitely loved having no interruptions. Bea only ruined his dreams of ever becoming a teacher. She brought pain into his life for sure, but she didn't get her to kill him. The professor was definitely going to be next on my list, after I was done with Mrs. Saunders.

"Illek was the whole reason we left. She was a controlling bitch, but she didn't have enough of him to wrap around her finger. We left because of her, but he died because of us. We both got the call; I didn't pick up the goddamn good-bye call because I'd just gone to sleep. God, why can I still hear the sound of his neck breaking?"

My reflection started to hold me back from my decision. "A reflection was something that reminded me of pictures; and pictures are only made for my dreams to have a familiar image to etch inside my head. Without pictures history isn't made, a belief for those who only believe in sight. I believed in what I saw. *His face, his eyes were open, and the image was burned inside my head. Why did his eyes have to be open? He looked at me like I had failed him as a friend.* I could only see what I believed, and I believed what I saw. I had to experience it. And these goddamn reflections were making me think about ending this before I got to her, but I couldn't. I was just too far in."

Languid, lethargic, loosely put together.
Unenergetic, unhurried, unemotionally guarded.

I convinced myself that this was supposed to happen. I just didn't know it would feel so empty.

Chapter 62

WHEN I APPROACHED the coffee shop I circled around it six times, and I finally got out of the car and came like a storm to an old, rusted, ramshackle lighthouse. I came closer and closer to her, and she was paralyzed at the emotionless human body advancing toward her.

I came to the table operated by a dark, troubled woman who didn't know who she was anymore. I came beside her. The proximity proved her illusion of safety in me. She should not trust me. I didn't even trust me.

"Now what is it that you wanted to tell me?"

"You don't even want work our way up to it? You just want to get straight to it." Oddly, this woman seemed like she was comfortable, and this was going to be a coffee talk kind of conversation.

"You have to understand my rush to end it." As she nodded, I knew that my disclaimer had made her comfortable enough to carry on.

"You just thought that I was some kind of murderer from the start, didn't you? You knew. I could tell you knew by the way you looked at me."

"No ma'am. I like to get to the truth through the idea that

everyone is guilty before they are proven innocent. If only our court system would work this way. I don't make assumptions; I get facts from the evidence." I lifted up the book with the confessions of Jesse. Confessions of everyday life that she would probably want to read. "I didn't know Jesse until I read this and became him. It said all of the things that you pressured him into doing. It told of all the suspects and every amount of damage they caused. They pushed him too hard." *They barely knew him.* They were to blame for this crime. This book was how I really knew him. Other than that, I knew him superficially. I should have known him better than I did, considering he was my roommate.

Chapter 63

SHE PUT THE book down still trying to keep her composure. She looked like she was looking for a way out of this, instead of confessing like she said she was going to do. *This angered me.*

"Why are you bleeding?" It's time for the truth. She needed the ugly truth because before she died by my hand, she had to feel guilty. She had to feel the guilt I experienced. When I still saw his face with his eyes open, he was staring at me with such distain.

"I bleed because you made Jesse bleed. His arms leaked like a sieve because of what you did that night, and what you've done his whole life. You won't get away from this accusation. It's in the writing. Nothing you can say or do can change writing. Anything you do can't be justified unless there are cameras. Anything you say can't be justified until it is written or recorded. I have this recorded confession, and I have the writing. I have all I need for my assurance."

"How did Jesse bleed from my hand?" She knew what I was talking about; she just wanted to pause the inevitable. Just like Illek. *How could a nurse not see my scars on my arms? She knew where it came from. She didn't want to believe it. She didn't want to believe that she didn't have control over his pain. 'Guess what? I'm not your puppet;*

243

I'll stand on my own.'

"Jesse did not bleed from your hand. He bled from the missing part in his life, a maternal leader. You were so caught up in your success you didn't cut any time for him. So he cut his own time. Time kills us all, but your lack of time for him killed more than just yourself. You killed a future for many people to be inspired by, for many people to listen to his words, and lastly you killed someone who was the Jesus of our modern day. You killed a perfect man. I bet if you could, you would go back. I bet if you could, you would change. I bet if you could, you would have stopped this from happening. But you didn't. You made the choice, and with every choice there is a path you take, and some paths are one-way, and you can't turn around. Life is like a voice mail, you can't take anything back. You can't start over. What's done is done. You are responsible for this damage. Now it's our turn to take this one-way path."

When she became perturbed, I felt invincible. I felt like I had brought justice to a never-ending, dark investigation. In the dark, I received light. I have found a light that could put me to rest. But she stopped. Her confidence was coming back. She felt like she had never done anything wrong. "I wanted to help him, but I had to punish him for what he had done. It was his fault for drinking. I never wanted my son to be a felon. I had to show him that this behavior was unacceptable."

"Well damn, you showed that pretty well. He's dead now. Is that the punishment you wanted? Is that enough to justify your check for life insurance?"

"Stop! I never wanted to receive any money. I never wanted to bury my son. My son was supposed to bury me. He did this, and I didn't know what to do."

"No!" I screamed as loud as I could as she became squeamish. People were watching and moving away from our propinquity. "You will not put this back on him. This is all because of you! You will not run away from this! You will not forget this, and he will never forgive you. For the very last thing he said to you was an unanswered I love you and good-bye. How can you justify what you have done with punishment? You're just like Professor Bea. Can't you see? You killed him. He is dead! Never again will you ever see your son."

"Stop. Stop. Stop. Why are you doing this to me?" Her confidence faded, and my fire burned.

"Always about you." I forced my bloody arms down on the table. I probably could have broken it if I tried harder to make more of a scene.

I calmed down and said, "I read about each person in his life that made him feel like dying. Beside your name it says, 'I thank the escape it brings me from her, and I curse the scars that the people see.' How does that make you feel? Does it make you take a couple steps back?" "There's more. 'I needed this escape. I needed to feel the physical pain so I could deal with the emotional pain she brought to me.' I have become Jesse in the last couple weeks. I haven't slept since I saw him." The next scream was all of my built-up anger that came out like a champagne bottle shaken up and opened. "LOOK WHAT YOU'VE DONE! YOU DON'T HAVE A GODDAMN CLUE WHAT YOU'VE DONE HERE! THIS ISN'T OVER LADY. YOU CAN'T SAY STOP, AND IT'S OVER! IT'S NOT OVER UNTIL YOUR LAST BREATH SAYS GOOD-BYE." I paused because I felt like I looked like a rabid dog. The veins in my head brought this feeling of explosion." It's not over until lonely, you remain."

"Why? Why is this happening? I thought you just wanted to talk. Why can't you see my remorse?"

What a stupid fucking question. There's no remorse in your voice. *What about your voice before this happened?*

"You are not getting past the evidence I have stacked against you. Just confess!"

"You're bleeding so much. You need some help. Someone help

him." Her attempt to bring attention away from the fact she was preparing her confession. I knew I was so close. I could taste it in her words. Everyone was gone on the outside tables. I needed to do it here or take her back soon before it wasn't my decision anymore.

"I bleed because Jesse bleeds. I cut because Jesse cut for all of you. I am becoming closer to death because Jesse has reached his." I can't stop laughing inside. *Always laugh, because if you can't, you shouldn't be doing it. Well I'm laughing with bleeding arms and a heart that beats off of the dead air filling my lungs.*

I found laughing on the inside gave me an edge when I was competing with someone in an argument. I was laughing to find the bright side of this suffering. It was scary how much I had become Jesse. Every time I said Jesse, it choked her hard, repetitively. *I knew she was scared of me now.*

"Jesse wouldn't. Why would he? He had a great life. This was an accident." Laughter quickly ended as the ignorance of her response was eating at me.

"If this was an accident, why did you call me?" I am the only one investigating this case. To everyone else, this is over, and it is just a normal death of a good kid. Nobody gives a shit about him now except me. *But this wasn't always the truth.*

I should have driven.

"You were beginning to admit it. So just say it."

Chapter 64

WE BOTH CALMED down. She became more susceptive to my conversation. No one ever said they were done with the conversation until I was done. I had a gift of disabling the ability to turn away from me. I was a car accident on the highway where everyone stopped to see if there was blood. I started to grin at the thought of having this control over her. I was laughing again.

"Jesse, I'm sorry you have to hear this, but I have to get rid of the grief." As if that were possible. "I'm sorry I wasn't the best mother to you." She uttered in a small voice that still looked up to the sky like something was there to speak back to her.

I haven't looked up in a while.

"Please proceed to your confession."

"I feel as if I am responsible for not caring and not being present in your life. I pressured you so much and was never there to see you succeed." She left him for months at a time. She was a bad mother. Her negligence would haunt her until justice was given. "When you called I was already having a bad day at work and I took it out on you. I had been working on a business plan for months and had it turned down. I worked so hard for that plan that it really made me sad to see it not work out." It was eating me alive. This bitch was as selfish as Illek. Stop the bullshit and speak the truth!

I became bored with this confession. I wanted to hear the truth, not the polite lies that she intended to sound good. My eyes said exactly what I was thinking. She knew that she needed to move on.

Chapter 65

"It was so late, and it was the last thing I wanted to hear. It was the only time you ever asked for money, and we decided not to give it to you because we thought you needed the punishment. You were never a drinker." That was where her confession started to hurt me. "Ever since your accident you never drove emotionally. You did both of those that night. That was my greatest disappointment in you. Oh Jesse, why? God why? Not you. You were supposed to outlive us. You were supposed to bury us, not the other way around."

I became really ill with her now. "Look, get to the point. Stop trying to make yourself look better. Jesse was murdered because no one answered the damn phone. You were the only one who could talk him out of it. Why didn't you stop him? He was drowning, and your idea of making him a better person was a punishment that ended his life."

"This is so hard." She placed her hands over her face, and the rest of her conversation was muffled.

"This is supposed to be easy? How easy was it for Jesse? How easy was it for him to do that to himself?"

"I know you didn't deserve this, but it seems like that turned into what happened and it happened because of me, and now your dad won't even look at me. I couldn't have known that this was going to happen like this. If I knew, I swear to God I would have done things differently. I am not capable of doing what you did, and trust me I have tried. I know it was hard to throw away your whole life. I guess I'm just too selfishly in love with my success. I would never be able to fill that void. I am not saying this because I think it makes you more of a man because you did that, but I am saying that there must have been a lot of things building up inside of you. I carried you off the cliff. You trusted me not to let you drop, and I let go. I let you go, and it is my responsibility to let you rest in peace, if that is at all possible. I can finally say that there is nothing worth living for any more without you here. I miss you, son."

"This is what we need." It was the darkest five-thirty had ever been in North Carolina. I knew what I had to do now.

"Is this what you wanted? Are you happy? I'm done." As she started to get up, I quickly sat her back down. She thought it was over. I started to grin, and I looked at her with my half-squinted eyes. She was not leaving this table without me. She was in my command, my control.

"And I asked myself why me? But I did not want to show any sort of self-pity. I'm not sorry for myself. But what did I get for being your friend? Look at what I am doing for you. Look at what I am doing to myself. Is this what I asked for when you became my friend? Is this what it means to be your roommate? Is this what it feels like to be responsible? I am not doing this to somehow keep your pride. I am doing this because they told me there was nothing left. *They murdered you. I murdered you.* This isn't over. Not yet."

"What do you mean?" She was so confused. She thought she had escaped it all by saying what she said. Little did she know that she just opened Pandora's Box. She should be scared of me now.

"Do you feel better now? Is it over for you? This won't be over until there is no more shame in Jesse's name." I started laughing again, and it started to show on my face. My eyes got extremely big when she looked at me.

"What do you mean by shame?"

I had to grin because I knew she wasn't ready to hear this, "Are you scared of me yet?" My laughter leaked out onto my face. She didn't have a clue what it meant to confess to this crime. She was not going to be willing at first, but she would eventually come to a consensus with her fate. *My fate. The fate I created from the start of this whole investigation.*

"Am I seriously awake right now?" She wanted badly to believe that she was not walking with me to her end. She wanted to feel safe! My face told her that there was no more safety for her, just forever.

"This is no dream." I saw that she was paralyzed sitting in her chair. She could not move. I had her right where I wanted her. She could not escape my undeniable truth. She was the weight pulling the rope that was sinking on the impact of my words.

"Where are we going?" She was trembling, and the shallow wind coming out of her vocal cords spoke nothing but fear.

"We're going to where Jesse's last breath was. We're going to where the last call was made to you. You left his call unanswered." I picked her up by the arm violently, so I could draw a crowd. A crowd was what I needed. It had to be good timing, and the timing couldn't be any more perfect. Probity was coming for both us.

Chapter 66

SHE WAS SUBMISSIVE to my voice now. She was not fighting back anymore. She opened the door and climbed into the car without a single word. I was confused. *Maybe she really thought this was her fault?*

Thinking about her giving in like she did, it started to make me rethink my whole strategy. I thought this would require me to convince her physically to give in to me. I wasn't used to someone actually agreeing with my vision, or helping in my cause. *Am I sure I want to do this now?* I started to break down, so I had to take a minute to gather my thoughts. It felt like getting an erection, just because my body wanted me to. No matter what I tried this erection wouldn't go away. My inquisition of manipulated thoughts drove me to my insanity. I was so goddamn conflicted that I had outbursts coming from the caged brawl inside my head.

I fought my thoughts. I didn't want to have them. Unfortunately, if anyone tells someone not to think about something, they're not only going to think about that something, but they will think about solely that one image that they used to represent that something someone said not to think about. My brain calmed down. I collected my aspiration for finishing this case when I finally got in the car. *Lock the doors and protect anything else trying to stop this from happening. This is what we want. This is what we need. Right?*

I was looking down at my feet in a subconscious way, almost afraid of the words coming next. "You are the first one to receive the pain from Jesse's death because you were last one he called. I will bring justice to his death through every single person who could have stopped this from happening; even myself. Every one of the suspects in his death, had some kind of role in this murder because we were all given the chance to end it. While we were blind to the outcome, we still all had the ability to end this before it started." She was startled to think about how I was responsible and I was still laughing as I knew my *fate* was not decided for me. I was my own puppet master. I controlled everything that was about to happen.

"Why can't I feel anything? Why does this make me feel like I'm dying? Where are we going?" Her once submissive attitude started to fade away as her voice became defiant. It was still funny to hear her speak in such a rhetorical way. She knew she was going to die. She was prepared to die. She just needed to know why. I was going to show her.

"I'm giving you what you want, your son back. Take my hand. My hand will take us both where we should have been from the start of this. I will show you what forever feels like, so maybe then you will know the damage you and I have caused. My purpose was to not go down alone. You are the reason I am going down in this fashion."

This silence tasted like dead air. The mixture of misled expectations and the awkwardness of waiting for her response consumed the car. *Had she only had a relapse of defiance?* Whichever one it was, nothing came from her voice again until we got to the place where it all ended. When I drove past the campus shops, I could tell people knew already. I wondered if I would get to the end of the list before they tried to stop me. *Why can't they let me make this right?*

The people already knew, but I felt like they were invisible and the scripted ending was invincible. None of them staring at us would matter in a few moments. I parked the car into the garage behind the hot dog shop, but this time I parked in another spot.

It was that busy time of the day; any time from the forty-five to five after minute of every hour was active because either a class was ending or beginning. I had to park on the fourth floor of the parking garage. I knew that people would be watching us from their apartment windows. I knew people would hear us both. All of those people's voices telling me that I was responsible for Jesse's early death would be silenced; even a moment of sincerity would be enough to hang the noise. They would make a rope out of the things I said to them. It would be my pleasure to see them all hanging from it. It all depended on how you looked at life to see who won. I looked at the reflection in the lake. Everything else was upside down. I took my life in their world, and I would get to watch their bodies dangle from the noose. Everything I did to myself would be verified through watching them all die as I took the lives of the two people most responsible for this disaster. I liked the way I looked at the world. It had been so much easier to hurt them because I controlled the skin they saw upside down. I controlled the knife to my skin. They could not do anything but make the reflection in the water. The only difference between medicine and poison was in the dose, so when they thought they were healing, I was killing their reflection. It was like I was looking at a glass half full and half empty; I saw past the image and felt the stress of emptying the rest of the glass.

Chapter 67

I HAD A tearing grip on her arm, and we started running to my room. I knew that I had to be giving her bruises on her arm. I squeezed her arm harder than the young man receiving needles to numb the pain of his broken ribs. People were staring at us. I probably would be staring too if I wasn't the one dragging a woman viscously down the street.

There was whispering amongst the audience, but I couldn't hear them. They were jumping in front of us to stop me, but I couldn't see them. They were trying to grab me, but I couldn't feel them. I was the dead, walking. I carried with me the stench of death and the taste of revenge.

I walked back up the stairs that I came down from less than an hour ago. The stairwell was clear this time. Nothing was going to stop me because this was a sign that what I did was right. The echo of her dangling body hitting the stairs repeatedly reminded me that I was supposed to be laughing. "Stretch your legs to coffin length Mrs. Saunders." My eyes nearly exited the sockets they laid in. Her face looked defeated and defenseless.

I was outside myself now.

I stopped in front of the messy door with a dry-erase board that sat on the outside. There were markings from a roommate who no longer tended the room. I looked long enough at the board for her to see it. She broke down into more tears and reached for the markings left by her late son. I opened the door slowly, peeking through to my bed. Then I opened it a little further, still gripping her arm. My room looked organized to me. I knew where everything was and exactly why I put it there. I saw my desk. My desk was full of letters, journals, sticky notes, and last semester's class notes. We took a step inside, and I still looked over at his desk. Every time I looked for him at his desk, I saw him writing. He was writing that night he died. *They* took him from that very chair. *What is the point of being alive, if all I want is to be dead?* When I brought her all the way into the apartment she fell apart and dropped to her knees. The rope was still there because it was evidence from the murder. "Jesse died because of all of us. You are the first one to receive this freedom of letting it go, for it will never leave us until we reached forever. At least not until we feel what Jesse felt."

In my sick, demented mind, I went to my desk. I started writing down everything she said to me, 'I feel as if I am responsible. I'm sorry.' I looked back at Mrs. Saunders and grinned. *What were they going to say now?* This was never what they thought it was. Everyone told me I was wasting my time. They told me this was my fault. *Well, look now, I'm not the only one.* I don't know if it was the sound of her voice making the words as the pen wrote on the sheet of paper or my own internal hopes of what she was really saying. *It didn't matter to me anymore. I'm not the only one now, am I?*

I wrote down everything I remembered her saying. My pen furiously scribed my investigation with exact detail. *I cannot believe he was gone. 'I'm here because in my heart I knew you were telling me something when you gave me both letters. I love you man.'*

I began to pick up the heaviest things in my room because I could hear sirens from outside the windows. *They were probably walking up this way. They were probably evacuating the building because of me.* I sensed dominance in my presence, thinking that I was the reason behind all of this chaos. I flipped over my desk with the papers sliding off making an even bigger mess. The top of the desk toppled over the closet beside the door. I slid the heavier part of the desk like a football player at practice as my knees powered forward and the desk slammed into the door to barricade anyone from coming inside to stop us.

She started to move out of my way, and I could tell she was contemplating ways to get out of this situation. She positioned herself like she was going to make a run for it, but I kept a corner eye on her.

I pushed over the top of Jesse's desk that still had a printer on top. The printer shattered and pieces of it hit her. The top part of the desk was lighter than the bottom, so I put the top of the desk on top of his bed. I started to pull out Jesse's old desk, but I stopped. I saw his music albums and remembered that night he drove my car. I could hear the music in my head from that night he drove my car. *I wish these thoughts were some kind of time travel. I wish I could go back to change what happened.* It was like I looked at life in the rearview mirror of a car flipped over in a ditch and wrapped around a tree. No matter how mutilated I was now, the rear mirror showed me where I could have changed what happened. Like a scar, it was a constant reminder of what I wished I could take back.

I pulled the desk out more and watched her move towards the door again. With all of my strength, I pushed the desk toward mine. She dodged my attempt to stop her from leaving by jumping up to the bed.

"Get down!" I demanded because my nervousness prevented me from allowing her the advantage of higher ground.

She came down from the bed, obviously frightened from the assertion of my voice. She sat on the floor. "What do you want from me?" she said, facing me. She sat with one of her legs curled in under her body. I laughed because her attempt to leave this room died when she came in here. She could not leave until her body was wrapped with a heavy, black plastic bag zipped over her head; she would leave the way Jesse left this room.

I smiled. "Death."

Her head dropped and her eyes widened as she took a shallow breath. She needed to know why I insisted on killing her.

"Do you know what I've done? Do you know what it's like being the one with a finger pointed at your face?" My eyes opened wide; I pointed at her face. I knew that she wouldn't like it because no one liked a finger in their face. I think it might be something to do with the frustration of the receiver's eyes, because two eyes attempted to look at the object directly in front of them, causing them to break focus. She had a cross-eyed look at my finger. "You're lucky that I am the only one to get this blame. You won't know what it is like wanting so deeply to go back and trade places with him. You won't know how it feels to wake up every day, not wanting to wake up. You won't know what it felt like to cut myself every day I met someone who Jesse cut his arms for. You will never know how this ends after I finish my first responsibility. Now you'll understand what it's like to have people tell you it was your fault that Jesse is dead." She started to cry again, and her skin under her eyes became raw, making the rest of her face red.

"What are you going to do to me?"

"It's not what I am going to do to you. It's how you're going to pay for what you've done to Jesse. Look, this isn't for you, it's because of you."

We were on the floor facing each other. She sat Indian style as she looked at me. Her eyes tried to convince me to stop, but my love was weak. I could not help her anymore. I was the means to her end.

She looked away from my face and placed her hands on the floor. She lowered her body like a spring ready to shoot upward. She tried to get up and head for the door. Luckily my room looked like a disaster now, with things everywhere on the floor, or else she might have gotten to the door. She tripped on a box of tapes. I followed her upward motion and sprung toward her fallen body. I stood over her. I grabbed the book I turned my back on and hit her over the head. Without even thinking, I kept hitting her over and over again. I couldn't stop. My fire burned to the outside of my body. She laid there on the floor. Her back steadily began to rise and fall. My weapon broke apart as the cover separated from the book and pages flew out sideways. I was still swinging it at her with basically nothing in my hands. My fists, clasped with broken pages, continued to strike the back of her head. The book that told all of the sins and how to be faithful to a higher power broke the skin on the back of Mrs. Saunders's attractive head. She laid there motionless. She finally looked controllable, like Illek when Jesse cut himself.

I started to shove her around to wake her up. I felt for a pulse, and she was still alive but not conscious. I spoke to her anyway. "Mrs. Saunders, you will feel the pain of responsibility, the pain of guilt, the pain of suffering, the pain of loss, the pain of no control, the pain of life ending, and I will be in the passenger's seat because this is my fault as much as it is yours."

I took off my jacket and thought to myself. *I hated putting on a sport coat that I have not worn in a while. They always had cards, old funeral cards, a celebration of their life or what life they had. The last one I had was left on the ground, and I picked it up.* I wasn't even invited to come to his funeral. They wouldn't let me in. I had to watch him get buried from afar. Everyone told me it was my fault, and I couldn't convince them otherwise. I felt like I was speaking to him, but really it was just an open window. "Now you know that I admit it was my fault. But like I told you before, this wasn't a suicide, this was a goddamn murder. I, as well as five other people, am responsible for the death of Jesse Saunders. I know that! I know that he would still be alive if it wasn't for me. But now I have the other responsible person in his death. I drove him to his end, but she started this whole thing. You have to believe me now because I have the evidence. She killed Jesse!" I started to scream because I wanted them to pay attention to me. I wanted them to be watching the last one responsible for Jesse's death complete a swan dive from the fourth floor of this building. A swan dive done at its perfection is beautiful. The ways a person can manipulate their body to do flips, turns, twists and enter the water with merely the splash of an ant. That's all I was in this case, an ant. I was the ant that brought the boulder of responsibility down with me. No one thought this was a murder. They were stuck on suicide. I had both of the highest-ranking suspects in Jesse's death. Together we will make a big splash. The currents in the waters will capsize boats. Everything they thought about Jesse's death will be destroyed. *They will understand that we all look so good as we fall.* I will die with the evidence on my chest. I wanted the proof to show all of those people, the ones who called me the only reason Jesse died. I wanted them to feel what it was like to cut their wrists every time regret was too overwhelming. I wanted them to see what they did to me. And more importantly, I wanted them to see what they did to Jesse.

I looked down at all of the hard work I had done for this investigation. I found some papers scattered on the floor and picked them up. I found a sheet that was halfway written on, and I wrote down the rest of the evidence, clearly labeling papers and journals so that the officials could understand what the evidence was saying. Then I found the tape, *the dark voice recorder that continued to still be a mystery.* I thought Mrs. Saunders would wake up when I kept playing the voice mail over and over again. But she didn't. She laid there, and again I checked for a pulse.

Part VII

"DANNY?" I HEARD *them* at the door like wolves pounding and strategizing ways to get in. They didn't know what I was capable of. "What are you doing, Danny? Please let us in."

I spoke hard. I spoke so they could hear. I spoke so everyone would hear. There was no time for all of the others, not anymore. Even with the others still alive, everything was right in place. They had their own things coming to them. "The path of righteousness is true. Jesse's death was not a suicide. There were plenty of suspects and murderers in this case. I haven't made it to you all, but I will no longer be able to bring the evidence to those responsible. But it will soon come to them. I am the sick. I am the death. I am the abandoned. I am the responsible. I have finished my part in this investigation. You all should know what happens next." *The world looks better when you're falling into the pits of hell.*

"We've got a possible 187. Fourth floor, Cone apartments. Requesting a negotiator." The officer had a deep voice. He might have been the one who pulled us out of the car that night. *He better not come in here.*

"You should walk in the dark with a friend before you ever walk alone in the light. You should all know that now! No one in that

263

circumstance should be alone!"

"Danny! This doesn't have to be like this. I know it's hard to cope when a friend takes his own life. You have to realize that alcohol was the *devil* that brought him to his death, not Mrs. Saunders." He spoke like he actually cared about me. *He's lying to you Danny. He's lying so you will let her go. Don't give in. We have something to finish here.* I was torn. I had my back against the wall now that *they* were here.

"No! Those are lies. Those are the things that you want us to believe. I'm done with this decision. You walk through that fucking door, and we're gone."

"Danny. Open this door. Everything will be okay, I promise." Promise ... how was I supposed to believe his promise without even knowing him? *Because he's lying. That's his job.*

Journal Entry

'Illek,

'You were the love of my life. You were the one who tried to change me and I failed. I failed you and you failed yourself. I'm reading one of your Valentine's Day cards and your last words were, "I love you and I'm sorry we fought on your favorite day. You have taught me so much and I want you to know I love you. I hope there are many more Valentine's Days to come." I don't feel like I have helped you at all because you never changed. Learning is observable through a change in behavior and I saw nothing but brief single moments of sincerity and the eventful relapses you had. You are not a terrible person and I do not want you to think this is for you. I am not doing this for you; I am doing this because my whole life fell apart tonight. My whole life fell apart when I couldn't even look at myself in the mirror. When I was behind a jail cell, I realized you were a big part of my life. You are the reason I made so many of the decisions I made. I'm sorry I cut myself in front you. I had no control over anything when you were angry. I did this for your attention. And don't worry, it wasn't really the first time I did it. I have done it before because of my mother. After I knew a way to get your attention, it became my romantic addiction. I did it for everyone

265

I loved. I did it because I wanted to change something that could never be altered. They say, "A fool never changes," but I say a fool wants to change something that happened. I am the fool that will pay the price of life. I don't want this anymore. I can't take the pain I have caused myself and to all of you. This is my way out. When I think of you as I prepare my fall, I will think of all the times you were my jelly bean. The times when your legs spasms with mine. I will forget the past that I don't want to remember and I suggest you do the same. You can't control what I am doing right now and resentfully enjoy it. I don't know if I am sick or if this was the way he wanted me to go out. Either way I won't capitalize his pronoun. I don't believe in him anymore. I lived a life he wanted me to live and it killed me. My mom always wanted me to be religious and I tried. I tried to do everything she told me to do. I have no bright memories of her to remember. My father is even more distant than before. He does not understand me. None of them do. You did. One memory I will take with me to my grave is how fun each Christmas was at your house. Your parents loved me. I didn't understand why they would give me not only the physical gifts under their tree, but also the gift of love. They cared about me and wanted me to be what I wanted to be. I loved the way I felt with them. I felt like they were so proud of me and would always be proud of anything I ever did. They loved that I wanted to be a teacher and I love them for that. I do not think I can ramble any more about us and our families than I already have so I will end this letter. If you telepathically get this message before I do this, then please stop me. I'm begging god to give me a sign, a reason not do to this. The broken crate is not enough. I need a true sign. I love you and goodbye.'

'Dan the man,
'I can't take this anymore, man. I know you would probably never guess that I was this bad. My life just seemed like it wasn't mine

anymore. Like I couldn't live the way I wanted to live. Everything I loved was stacked up against me. I can't take the pain anymore. I hope no one thinks this is your fault. No matter what they say, don't let them hurt you. Stay true to yourself always and life is easier to live. This isn't your fault, it's mine. I wanted to help so many people that I forgot the first innate instinct of survival. I needed to help myself first. I really don't get it why I'm like this. My whole life as a kid I was always good by myself. I guess I never let go of the neglect of my parents. Don't let the little things bother you and never bottle anything up. I am about to do something I will not regret because I have been planning this for a long time. If you are reading this now, then I've completed what I set out here to do and no one can stop me. I feel like I have been coping with something my whole life. I cope with these hard things in life with sizable scars. I don't recommend this because it becomes addicting. I had control over one thing in my life and that was my knife. You have control over so much more. Please take what I've done as something you shouldn't follow. It has been a pleasure knowing you this year. As far as faith, I know you are a religious man, and I tried to believe, but I need a sign right now. I need you to wake up without a noise or a touch. If he wants to send me a sign then I want you to wake up as I write this down. I know he won't wake you up because he has never given me a sign before when I desperately needed one. When you do wake up and see me again, I want you to remember the good things about me and not this person I've become. If he is planning on doing anything then I want him to make you feel like it's not your fault. I want him to help those that have loved me, because they are the reason I am the way I am. I want you to meet people like them because they made me happy. I want him to tell them that this wasn't your fault.

'Well, I finished my ramble. You're still asleep. I didn't want this to be so easy. I want something to hold me back because I can't even delay the seemingly inevitable situation with a sign from god. I guess you'll wake up when you're ready. I love you and good-bye.

'Jesse'

Chapter 68

A LETTER SAT on the chest of a young man sleeping in a small apartment room. The single sheet of paper reeked from the truth of scars, folded with the crusted dark brown color of dried-up blood that's smeared along the face of the letter. The young man will not read the letter before he witnesses what will change his life, forever.

The young man woke up to a sound that would never leave his ears. He heard the sound of his friend's last breath as it jolted outward. The noise mimicked a squealing dog after it got slammed by a car going forty miles an hour. The sound echoed throughout the room. His vocal cords hid themselves as he screamed without even a single decibel produced from his open mouth. He saw a friend hanging from a rope around his neck. He choked on the lack of air that he kept trying to inhale. Death swallowed the young man whole. He dropped to his knees from the bed he slept on.

The young man had to look away before tears slowly fell. Everything his body was used to doing died that very moment he saw his friend. He kneeled toward the dangling body and gripped his legs. Finally, his body turned on again as he began to cry, sweat and beg for his friend to wake up.

The faint sound of his voice became the loudest he could talk,

"God. No. Jesse … smile." He grabbed higher up toward his friend's head. "Jesse. Why are you looking down? Come on man." His words stuttered when he started to pull at the body. "What's wrong? Why aren't you smiling? Please smile." His words became louder and louder. He screamed out, "AHHHHHHHH GODDDD. Why? Tell me why? No." The young man looked into his friend's eyes, and he yelled until his vocal cords bled inside his mouth. The young man moved his way up to his friend's arms. Blood covered them both now. "SSSMMMMIIILLLLEEE! Jesse, fucking smile man!"

The young man was lost. He was lost in a moment he chose not to leave, a moment where he wanted to do everything he could do to make his friend smile. He was lost at what to do with the body. He had never seen or heard anything like this before.

There was a room, a place where choices make changes. Every moment in that room was another chance to turn it all around; inside what seemed like hell was the clarity of only one choice to his friend. This room had the ability to change everything. It could've made new pathways of choice and decisions. It could have brought a new life. This room could have led to different endings. The choice became foreign to the young man, and the same room would become another turn of the sequence.

Chapter 69

"WHAT KIND OF friend was I to bail him out when his parents wouldn't? What kind of girlfriend takes him away from a situation that could have prevented all of this? What kind of lover would say it's over when she had been exposed to the love he had for her? What kind of friend selfishly pressures someone into doing something because he doesn't want to do it? What kind of teacher punishes someone by killing his dreams? What kind of friend drives someone to his death? What kind of parent creates this whole situation? And if I keep hearing that people make mistakes and this is just a speed bump in your life, I will kill them with my bare hands. If speed bumps were like all of the scars on my arm, then I guess I've been driving too fast over them. I have hit them too hard. I have done this to myself, but Jesse had people do it for him. Well, I guess Jesse's speed bump was tall enough for him to jump off with a rope around his neck. So don't speak of speed bumps when you talk about my best friend's life."

"Danny!" His raised concern in one last plea for me to stop proved that I was scaring him too. "You don't want to do this Danny ... Trust me!"

"Trust you? You're the whole reason he went over the edge! And how do you know I don't want to do this? Do you know what the FUCK it's like to wake up to find him like that!? Do you know what a true forever is? DO YOU! I know and I will show everyone what I am capable of. I am capable of bringing truth to this cluttered mess. Watch me!"

"Danny! No! Bring Mrs. Saunders out of this room and let's talk about this."

"That's all I've been doing for days upon weeks! Forgive me if I don't feel like speaking about this any more and allow this alibi to settle. Let me finish. Mrs. Saunders is fully content with the consequences of being held responsible for his suicide. She said it. She said I don't have a reason to live without him here. I will help her. I will help her forget about the pain. I helped her let go of Jesse. Now allow me to finish, so I can let go." *I knew past tense would make them wonder and they may even be a little more frightened that she was already dead.*

Chapter 70

THERE WAS A handsome silence as I built up this part of my speech. Everyone was listening and with the loudest scream and with all the windows open, I was allowing the wind to carry me out over the cliff. Unlike Jesse, I was begging for it to drop me.

"We have a murder victim and a possible suicide. Where's the negotiator?" I could hear him talking to his communication radio. I started to slam my fist on the desk that was blocking the door.

"It's way too late for negotiations. You can't stop me. You don't have control of this situation! I do. And she's not dead yet. But she knows what she did. She admitted the truth. I have the evidence."

I thought I heard words from a recognizable voice. *I was starting to question myself. Was I hearing things or was she really here?*

Mrs. Saunders was laying there on the ground like a rape victim who couldn't fight anymore. I was prepared to have my way with her. She'd lain there so quietly, as if she was already dead.

"This was my fault. I made him drive when I knew neither one of us should drive. My selfishness is the reason he is dead. I made him drink when he didn't want to have anything to do with it. Jesse, being so naive and so easily convinced, fell to my desire. He drove, and it was people like you who will feel the pain that the

people from the list will feel. You are just as responsible in this suicide as anyone else on the list."

"What do you think Jesse would say about this? What the hell
does it prove, Dan? By ending this cycle, you are about to start
another one, man. Come on!" His words worried me. I was actually
analyzing what he was saying. That meant I was actually listening
to him. *Stop Danny! You know what you have to do, SO DO IT! This
is what we have been working on for so long. End it! End her! End the
pain that has followed us!*

"Stop speaking!" I had Jesse's voice as a play over on my voice. I
was speaking to both of them, the officer and myself. I was loud. I
was finally forgettable. I was ready for forever.

I knew it would happen like this. She would become so beautifully red. First a running red necklace would quickly turn into a
dress. I opened the window of the last room I would breathe in. I
had prepared my last speech. I was going to speak the same last
words as Jesse, I love you and good-bye.

They were so close now.

Chapter 71

I SPOKE SOFTLY and quickly, "When his parents wouldn't bail him out because they wanted to punish him, they brought him over the edge, to a drop that would kill anyone, and I was the stop to the wind. I stopped him from floating. I aided his end. I dropped Jesse. They put Jesse there, and I let him drop to his death. I had to be the first one to see the product of my work too. I can still hear his fucking neck breaking. It's a sound that will never leave my mind. I didn't know he was even capable of doing what he did. No one did. He was so happy. He had a life of love for anyone who walked in it. I am graced with knowing Jesse for the length of time I knew him. I have a job now and I must finish it. I am going to become my own end."

They were banging at the door, speaking all at once, and I couldn't hear anyone. I bet all of his suspects were watching now. This is what I needed. The other suspects had no way of physically stopping this, so they must watch. The ones who had a chance to physically stop him from doing this, are about to die.

"His mom got the call that explained what happened. She got the first call. He couldn't have been thinking about forever. Not until after that conversation. It must have been her fault. I didn't need to justify that she could have physically stopped this, because she had tried many times to do what I was going to do for her. She could have stopped this from the beginning when she decided not to pay the money for him to come out. And I could have stopped him at the end of his life. I drove him back after paying his bail. He only needed time to come back to his original self in a jail cell, his happy personality that we all took for granted. *I should've stayed with him. But I ran away when they took him.* Now we must pay for our debts. He called every one of you." I had a crowd now. I felt like the world was watching. "I came into this whole investigation with the full intentions of dying for it." I couldn't be a hundred percent sure they were watching, but I had a good feeling that this story would be heard by them forever. "Seeing is believing, in the eyes of those who have no faith. Jesse's death has rid any faith I ever had. The Christian people would say it was his time to go. Well how the fuck is He supposed to know when it's the right time for someone? What does faith in God have to do with fate? I don't have control over this situation? Is that what you're saying? I think I made it pretty fucking clear I had control over this now. I don't have faith in fate. But I do have faith in death as the only true meaning of forever. To bring back a moment that could have changed this whole story, I would cut my throat for it."

"I know you must think I am the one who is most responsible, and all of the people who heard the story have told me that thousands of times, but now I have proven this wasn't a suicide. This was a murder, and I, as well as the five other people he called that night, was responsible. But none of you are as responsible as me. And no one knows what it's like." I broke down. I'd held it together until this very last moment.

"Danny we're coming in." They were about to feel the door slam back into them because I put the dresser and flipped over the bed in front of the door. They should only have a small space to reach an arm through, but no one would able to come in.

"He didn't need a reason to kill himself. He wanted a reason to live." They stopped trying to bang their way in when they heard me speaking again. I could hear the officer telling the other wolves to hold their position. He wanted to hear what I had to say.

"Think about your family. What will they think of this?" *I wish he didn't say that, so I pretended like I didn't hear him.*

"Do you know what it's like? Do you! Do you know how it feels to be the reason for someone's death? Do you know what it's like to see your friend hanging from a rope with wrists ripped apart from his skin? DO YOU KNOW WHAT I'VE DONE? None of you know because none of you are as responsible as I am now. So, like Jesse said to each one of the six, GOOD-BYE." The wind was going to let me go. As I fall, I would hear every branch break as there was no stopping me from dying, like Jesse. First things first, she had to die. When I put the knife up to her throat, I heard something, a voice. *What have I done?*

Something spoke and it sounded so familiar.

"Dan. I'm here. It's going to be okay." The voice seemed so passive and defeated, but I couldn't proceed until I heard her again.

What was she doing here? Cut her throat Jesse. Do it! Don't delay. They're coming in now. Rip her apart!

"Dan, just open the door. I'm here for you." *Why was she here?*

I felt the muscles in my arm holding the end of her life melt. She was unconscious. *What have I done?*

"It's going to be okay. Danny, please talk to me? Please? Let me know you're in there." I felt my joints slowly start to release. My body was shutting down. She was the only one in the room who didn't feel like they had to be abrupt and rushed to try to talk me out of killing her.

Why were these things, these words, these lies, affecting me? Cut her throat and make this right. All of these decisions were becoming the pouring water reaching my neck. I dropped to the floor next to her. I was so close to her I could only see her out of one eye, and even that was blurry. When thoughts stopped in my head I had become at peace with myself, like the time I went to Spain, like the time I walked into Georgio's office, like the time Illek healed me, like the time I deleted the message before it finished.

That was something that hadn't happened in a while. I briefly felt the calming of my body. My shoulders relaxed and it felt phenomenal. It's not until you know the deepest exhaustion that you feel the utmost rest and relaxation.

I could hear the door open. I had to make a decision. The voice was coming through again. Relentless couldn't describe how much she was delaying this from happening. *How did she know to come here? How was she able to make me feel like she was taking my hand away from Mrs. Saunders?*

I was burying my teeth into the floor. I couldn't hear a word coming out of her mouth, but I could see what she was saying. She said it over and over again. "You've got your savior. She is here. She's here for you. She is here for you because I wasn't there for him. Open the door." I laid there. I knew that I had a way out. I had only one idea this whole time, one feeling, one taste, one deception. I was backed in a corner I put myself in. I was trapped, but now I have a choice. She was here.

They were smart. They didn't come barreling in here, at least not yet. When she came through the door, I was on my feet. When she came towards me, we said nothing. She came close to me, trying to overlook my scars and the cuts on my wrists. By that point, I was too. She looked at the figure lying on the floor. She blinked her eyes for longer than a normal person would because she was relieved that Mrs. Saunders was still breathing. She knew she was still alive. Then she came closer to me. *She was sent in. From whom?*

A hug. It wasn't like I never had a hug from someone before, but the unusual length of this hug spoke a thousand words that neither individual could say with words. I almost dropped the knife and realized someone answered my call. *If I would've gone through with my plan, who would have been responsible then?* It wouldn't have solved anything. I would've started this all over again. I knew something had to collide to stop this constant spinning of cycles. I had a reason to live and forever will have to wait until I'm ready. I not only had control, but I also had a choice. I was still gripping the knife, but my grip was slipping.

It was like one of those moments where you don't want to leave, but you are only thinking about all the ways to keep it going instead of living in that moment. There was an alternative, a different path for me. I let go of the knife and any fear of the future. I relaxed. This could have ended in so many different ways, but I had the help to let me stop this cycle. She collided into this room. She was the wall to my circling wind. She stopped me.

In reality no person can make you do anything. No situation can force you to do something. All of that power is invested in your thoughts, and the way you act on it is your decision. The quote, "The sky is the limit," seemed wrong now. No external force can limit something from us. The mind sets the limit, and it can be pushed past boundaries or stay secure inside them. Not one of those people I spoke with were responsible for what happened. We all have a choice. It doesn't have to be limited or pushed by the wind.

Chapter 72

THERE WAS A room, a place where everything could change in an instant. Where moments of uncertainty become the disambiguation of what happened. Dreaming became a reality, which left reality doubtful.

The young man stood there with arms around the only reason reality didn't seem so terrible. Although he turned his back on faith, he no longer believed in coincidence. Danny sank deeper and deeper into an abyss. Without question, there will always be a time where sinking becomes the only feeling left. Through all misfortunes there seems to be a sweeping undertow, which presents itself with tactical reasoning, high waters, and a sturdy current. There are moments when man is solitarily inept. Something pushed him back out of the drowning water. And he will never forget how that room saved him. Everything he thought about life changed. He became a believer.

CPSIA information can be obtained at www.ICGtesting.com
Printed in the USA
LVOW041544261111

256546LV00002B/29/P